"]

Heartbreaking for the parishioners, what's left of them anyway. Cardinal's trying to convince us to combine with St. Margaret's over on the west side. Never happen."

She turned to the altar, aimed quickly, and snapped a single picture.

"I heard."

"We're hoping the Archdiocese reconsiders, what with the history and beauty you've just seen. I hope you include that in your story. Subtly, of course. No quotes or anything."

"Which one's the Madonna?"

He bowed his head, raised an arm weakly, and started toward the side altar. She passed him and stopped. He caught up.

"Would you like to light a candle, Ms. Feldman?"

She stared down at the bank of votive glasses, most of them empty, glass blackened, burnt wicks lying on the bottom. Two contained lit candles, one flickering, threatened by the liquid pool of wax it created. She drew a long taper from a holder, caught flame from the weak candle, and lit a fresh one.

He searched his pocket for change and found none. He placed his empty closed fist on the coin slot of the offertory can and shook the whole thing. The change inside rattled.

"Father, tell me about the miracle."

"Pardon?"

She looked up at the statue. "When Victor Rodriguez's body was found, the statue was crying."

"Who told you that, Ms. Feldman?"

"I heard the tears were red, like blood."

Ocean Park

by

Michael Walsh

The Ocean Park Series

Ocean Park

Cover Art by *Diana Carlile*

The Wild Rose Press, Inc.
PO Box 708
Adams Basin, NY 14410-0708
Visit us at www.thewildrosepress.com

Publishing History
First Mainstream Mystery Edition, 2015
Print ISBN 978-1-5092-0364-2
Digital ISBN 978-1-5092-0365-9

The Ocean Park Series
Published in the United States of America

Dedication

To Jean,
love of my life

Chapter 1

Another corpse had been discovered in the Church of St. Ambrose, the second in a month.

Detective Matt Conley snapped the collar of his leather jacket up against the wind, exhaled a frosty breath, and heaved the oak door open on the church's vestibule. Tonight it was as dark as a confessional.

"This ain't right," Eddie Jackson said, stepping in behind him and rubbing his palms together as if preparing to pray. "Church ain't a place for dead people, and on a Sunday no less."

"Really? What about funerals, Eddie? Been a couple of those in the hundred years of St. Amby's."

Jackson rested his head against the wall and folded his arms. Two lumps under his parka suggested breasts, but Conley knew the left bulge was a service revolver, the right one a pint of wine or Jim Beam. The choice depended on whether it had been a bad day or a real bad day for his partner.

Conley yanked the interior door open on the old church. Dusty yellow street light drifted in through the Stations of the Cross in the stained glass windows, past Jesus carrying his cross, past Mary, Simon of Cyrene, and the centurion. Light barely reached the wooden pews, their armrests and tops curled like dark waves rippling away from the altar. The altar was pitch dark, but the curved ceiling was discernible—painted clouds, blue skies, and saints in flowing robes.

A click sounded behind him. The narrow beam of a flashlight swept the pews.

"Smell him?" Jackson asked, waving the light too fast to distinguish anything. "Smells like fresh hamburger. No mistaking that stink. We ought to fine the priest, you know. Second time this month a homeless bum croaked in here. Unsafe as hell. Priest gotta lock the damn door."

"So the homeless can die safely in the gutter, right?"

Jackson grabbed his arm. "Don't need your fucking wisecracks. Keep it up and I'll get you transferred to Vice. How'd you like to round up fags in the bus station shithouse?" he snarled, his face inches away.

Sweet, candied breath told Conley this was a Jim Beam night. He shrugged off the hand and continued forward.

Jackson was an ugly drunk. He'd gotten the two of them in scrapes more than once, fights Conley always had to finish alone. The only fighting Eddie ever did was for a bartender's attention.

Jackson snorted, walked to the other side to search, and called over his shoulder, the cavernous building amplifying his voice just as it was designed to do. "Doesn't matter, Matt. They're closing this place in four months anyway. By May it'll be a roller rink or a nightclub. Maybe they'll hire me as a bouncer when I retire."

I can hardly wait.

The unheated church felt colder than outside. Its stillness captured the New England winter bite and held it with marble and thick wood and dark walls. Conley walked the main aisle slowly so his eyes could adjust, and touched the top of each bench, wood worn smooth by the countless touches of Ocean Park Catholics, people who found solace in fairy tales.

He'd been one of them—once.

Jackson's noisy shuffle stopped and his flashlight clicked off. A bottle cap rasped as it was unscrewed. A pause, a contented sigh, another rasp. The light clicked back on and washed aimlessly around the quiet church.

Conley was halfway to the altar now, parallel with the window of Christ receiving his crown of thorns. He had enough night vision to see the rail guarding the altar, enough to see a dark form in the first row, right next to the aisle. An important seat, that one—sometimes functional, sometimes ceremonial. Funeral directors commanded it, along with fathers of the bride and generous, self-important parishioners who must have slept through the gospel on humility.

He slowed. His partner approached from the other side of the church and settled his light on the dark hulk.

They each stopped at the end of the aisle and waited a beat as if doing the step-pause procession wedding parties were taught. Conley walked wide until he touched the red leather top of the wrought iron altar rail where St. Ambrose's faithful had knelt together for a hundred years, elbows planted in the plush cover, chins thrust forward for communion.

Jackson's unsteady flashlight flickered on the sitting body. Conley saw mostly darkness, a head, and an outline of formidable shoulders and chest. He reached the middle of the rail. Felt the latch to the gate that opened only for processions and spring cleaning. Waited for his partner to catch up.

Jackson shone his light on the person in the seat of honor. The body's head was canted back way too far, resting on the seatback because the neck had been carved open in a wide smile of gaping pink flesh that looked like toothless gums. Blood painted the front of a white shirt in a jagged semicircle, darkened a red-and-white striped tie, and made a black vest glisten.

Conley approached the body, right hand up to signal "don't move," an unnecessary gesture. Jackson was drunk, swaying like an Easter palm, his wrinkled eyes drawn to reptilian slits. Pasty jowls and a high forehead comb-over shone pale in the spill of flashlight.

A crash rang out to the left, echoing rolling thunder around the church. Jackson dropped his light and it clanged, shut off, and clattered away on the worn tiles.

"Gun!" Jackson cried as he ran the zipper on his jacket, and the sound of his pint bottle breaking on the floor followed the word like an added exclamation point.

"No! Eddie!"

Jackson answered with a bullet. A buzz whistled close to Conley's right ear. He dropped to the floor and rolled to the benches as breaking plaster pinged and metal clinked sharply.

"Eddie!" The sudden call brought more bullets— one into a window this time, more burying into plaster and lathe, another digging into wood with a sharp thwack.

Lights flicked on in the rectory next door. Conley knew Father McCarrick heard the gunfire, but hoped he'd call for help instead of entering the church.

Conley waited and listened. He knew the sacristies, and unless it had been the priest's or the altar boys' quarters that the intruder had entered, unbolting the heavily locked exit doors would be no easy task in the dark. Chances were he came in through St. Ambrose's front door and would have to leave that way.

But the intruder wasn't the immediate problem. Conley needed to take his partner's firearm away because every bullet Jackson fired increased Conley's chance of becoming the newest dead body in St. Amby's.

Sirens in the distance. He crab-walked behind Jackson, stood, and grasped his forearm. Jackson fought back weakly, free hand clawing. A sharp bam sounded, a bullet twanged, and the ceiling sky crunched. Conley took the gun, shoved Jackson to the floor harder than he should have, and moved toward the altar. The church was quiet save for his partner's muffled wheeze—until the hinges on the sacristy door squealed slowly. Steps tapped lightly and stopped at the side altar.

Conley called dispatch as he moved and requested backup in a whisper, knew he should wait for help, also knew he couldn't let the suspect leave. He shuffled toward the sound, kicked the lost flashlight, snatched it as it rolled. He rounded the pews in a crouch, gun pointing, and approached the side altar, which was as dark as the inside of the tabernacle it housed.

He pointed the flashlight. The big candleholder lay flat on the floor, tall white candles broken and scattered on the marble. A child crouched behind it, her long dark hair and black clothes a stark contrast to the bone-white foundation of the Madonna statue. The girl was olive-skinned and refugee thin, with Asian eyes that tracked him like a cornered cat's. She huddled closer to the stone base, a shivering creature curled into a question mark.

He fit the gun in the back of his waistband, laid the flashlight on the floor, and removed his jacket. She shrank farther away, pulling her high-topped sneakers under her. The flashlight lit the statue of St. Mary in flowing pastel robes—robin egg blue and flamingo pink, the nuns had always said—the life-size figurine that the little girls of St. Ambrose climbed wooden ladders to crown every May.

"It's okay," he said, opening his jacket. "Come."

The church's front doors opened. More flashlights. More voices.

"It's all right," he said to the girl. A drip splattered his bare forearm.

Jackson had composed himself and was standing at the entrance, calling orders to patrolmen. Doors banged. Men shouted.

Another drip made him look at the Madonna. Red tears ran from her pale doll eyes and sluiced between her plump plaster cheeks and noble nose like a grieving widow's mascara.

No way.

The girl uncurled and shuffled to him. He wrapped her in his jacket, felt her warmth. The patrolmen were close now, and Father's voice called a timid "Hello" from the sacristy. St. Ambrose's lights came on, illuminating the crying Madonna, and dragging Conley into yesterday.

The choir organ bursts into song. Mrs. Kelly reads sheet music through butterfly glasses, a dozen shrill voices fluttering behind her. Young Father McCarrick climbs to the pulpit. St. Ambrose's parishioners mumble "Peace be with you," and minutes later do battle on the church steps when Mass is over, hurl accusations, and sow the seeds of hatred that will last years, all over a piece of plaster.

He looked at the statue and shook his head.

"Not again," he whispered.

Chapter 2

The body was removed from the church on a gurney, its wheels clacking and squeaking. Harsh morning sunlight beamed through tall windows and revealed signs of St. Ambrose's age—yellowed wood, jaundiced marble, floors scuffed to a gritty gray. A forensics team searched the church for evidence. Jackson was explaining the broken bourbon bottle to a state cop, hands gesturing, the sweet smell of spearmint gum flavoring his words.

Conley stood near Father McCarrick and the statue of the Madonna. McCarrick nodded toward the young priest at the altar.

"He's a twit, that's who he is."

"I mean his name, Father. What's his name?"

Keeping Father McCarrick focused was never easy. His mind wandered, banked and dove like a fighter jet, braked and cornered like a race car.

He sighed. "His name is Father Francesco Spinelli. I call him Frank. He hates that."

"Why is he here? You never needed help at St. Ambrose."

"He's not here to help, Matt. He's here to harm. Frank is the Archdiocese man those morons in Boston sent to close St. Ambrose." He made a quick sign of the cross and genuflected. "He's a bean counter, making an inventory before we lock the doors."

8

Father Spinelli found the knuckle Jackson had shot off St. Michael the Archangel and held it to the saint's hand, inspecting the fit.

"The moneychangers finally made it from the vestibule to the altar," McCarrick said loud enough for Spinelli to turn and shake his head.

"So who made the call about the body, you or Father Spinelli?"

"I did, Matt. I did, of course. If Frank discovered someone here in the middle of the night, he'd pass the collection basket."

"But didn't you see the man was dead?"

"Matt, I just came into the sacristy to change a chasuble and stuck my head out to check the church. Never even put the overhead lights on. When I saw someone sitting in the dark, I called to him and he didn't answer."

"But he might have been sleeping."

"Yes, but last time I tried to wake a homeless person, they were frozen as a fish stick. Fell over on my leg and gave me a nasty bruise."

"So you called the police."

Father Spinelli had found the wooden May Crowning ladder and climbed the main altar to check the plaster behind the statue of St. Joseph. He poked his finger into a bullet hole in the wall.

"Yes, Matt. I called 9-1-1. Asked for you, in fact. St. Ambrose's needs one of its own sorting out this horrible tragedy. Besides, it was the only way I could think of to get you to visit your church."

Conley pointed at the Madonna. "What do you make of this, Father? More vandalism?"

McCarrick looked up at a policewoman in a white

9

lab coat brushing particles of the dried tears into a plastic cup.

"Miracles happen every day."

"It's not a miracle, Father."

"You said that awful fast, Matt."

Father Spinelli's ladder teetered and he held the statue's arm for balance.

McCarrick grinned. "Maybe St. Joe will fall on Frank. Another miracle."

"Father McCarrick," Spinelli called, voice shaking. "I need some help, please."

McCarrick cupped his hand next to his mouth and called, "God helps those who help themselves, Frank. I'm surprised you didn't know that."

A policeman ran to the altar and steadied the ladder as the young priest descended.

"I'm sure this is vandalism," Conley said, "just like the time Simon O'Neil painted chicken blood on the statue many years ago. I was young, never knew the whole story. Why'd he do it?"

"Because he's nuts, Matt. A crazy asshole." McCarrick stopped and crossed himself again, quick knee to the floor this time—almost to the floor. He sighed before he spoke.

"Simon did it because of me, you could say. When I took over I modernized things—guitars at mass, teenage rec center in the basement, BINGO two nights a week. O'Neil fought me every step of the way, wanted to keep the Church in the Middle Ages. An extremist. He thought he'd recruit St. Mary to his side. Gave her chicken blood tears, can you imagine?"

"What did he think that would accomplish?"

"Said he thought the tears would be a sign the

Blessed Mother was saddened by a modern St. Ambrose." The priest shook his head. "Intimidation and extortion. Terrorism, that's what it was. Religious terrorism."

"Do you think he did it again?"

"Who knows what that bird is capable of? I'll tell you one thing. He hasn't been to a Mass in twenty years at St. Ambrose. I'd know. Maybe he's taking communion at St. Margaret's with the rest of our traitorous parishioners."

"I'll have a talk with him, Father."

"I'd say send my regards, but I make it a habit not to fib when I'm standing directly in front of the altar."

"What about the girl, Father? Do you know her? Her name is Channary."

"Never seen the poor thing, but I recognized the tongue. Cambodian."

"I know. Health and Human Services is already looking for a translator."

"She probably lives down near the Saugus River, you know, where those Asians have taken over. Buddhists, all of 'em. Temple in the house and all that, can you believe it?"

Father McCarrick held the rail for balance, his knock-knees struggling to carry his five-foot-six, two-hundred pound frame. They passed the seat where the victim had been found, the man who'd been identified as Victor Rodriguez.

"How's Lisa, Matt? How's that business going?"

Business? You mean my marriage, Father? If it truly were a business, we'd be declaring bankruptcy.

The thought of his failing marriage tightened his throat.

"Fine, Father. We're working things out."

"It's not easy to lose a child. God's the comfort you need."

"Tell Him that."

McCarrick breathed a long sigh and laid his beefy hand on Conley's forearm. "Matt, I'd like you to be in charge of the investigation. The Church needs someone who'll fight hard to right this desecration."

"It doesn't work that way, Father. The Essex County District Attorney decides." Conley pointed at a man in a suit. "The D.A. assigned the case to the Massachusetts State Police. Captain Stefanos is in charge."

"But it's my church. I'm officially requesting you."

"I'll be on special assignment under Stefanos because I was first on the scene. That's protocol. But don't worry, the staties are lazy by nature. They rely on locals like me to do most of the work."

McCarrick nodded. "Good. We need someone who respects the Church, who knows its people. That's important."

McCarrick stepped out onto the small porch at the top of the steps to the sacristy. A frigid wind greeted them, wrapping the bottom half of the priest's cassock around his stubby legs.

"I'm so glad you're here, Matt. I'm worried. Very worried."

"About what, Father?"

"Something's wrong with Ocean Park, Matt. A priest learns a lot about what's going on if he keeps his ears open. My days are spent at wakes, weddings, family counseling…" McCarrick shrugged, lowered his voice—"gin mills, even. The life of the community unfolds like a Martin Scorsese movie—sometimes joyous, sometimes a glimpse of hell. Develops the instincts, teaches you to know things just by rubbing your belly."

He looked down at his ample belly as if he'd just discovered it.

"I think you're wrong, Father. Ocean Park is getting better. Don't give up on it. You're just upset because the church is closing."

McCarrick shook his head. "I don't think so, Matt, but I know those turkeys at the Archdiocese have made a very bad decision. Something's wrong. I feel it. Drugs. Gangs. Prostitutes. Murder in St. Amby's. Jerks like Father Frank poking around."

The breeze blew the priest's hair back and framed his round face in a fuzzy black halo, as the statue of St. Francis in the garden cast a long, dark shadow over them both.

Chapter 3

The whore opened the motel room door, the light snapped on, and Vithu clutched her collar, his fist full of red pleather and fake fur. Samay saw that the tattooed letters on the back of his mentor's fingers spelled LOVE. The irony wasn't lost on him—the whore suddenly sported a human-hand necklace that advertised her trade.

She almost escaped before Vithu slammed the door. In fact her hand was flat on the guest instructions—CHECKOUT AT 11:00. ICE MACHINE DOWN THE HALL. Samay and the eleven others, ethereal in a cloud of hash smoke, stood around a bed with a nappy ivory spread and watched Vithu trap the girl for bauk.

Bauk—the Cambodian practice of gang raping a prostitute, was the first initiation rite for the Ocean Park Asian Boyz. Samay found her surprise exciting, delicious, as if she'd stumbled onto her own party. But tonight the party was for him, and they were guaranteed privacy. Two Ocean Park policemen, paid off by Vithu, stood sentry outside the door, easy duty on a slow Monday night.

Seconds later the girl nodded, knowing her choices were rape or a beating—and then rape. Samay was glad. They'd already spent too much time waiting. Smoked a lot of hashish and drank sweet wine. Talked too much about gang fights and Pon, the legendary Asian Boyz gang leader traveling to Ocean Park from Long Beach.

Laughter rippled, surrounding the girl as she stripped with the resignation of a prisoner walking to the gallows. She lay on the sagging mattress. Pale skin peppered with freckles and moles. Samay was first, and though he was a stranger to white women and the company of others to so intimate an act, he had no trouble performing. His friends cheered, congratulated him when he was done, then jockeyed for their place in line. The girl's musk and sweat mixed with the sweet smoke.

There was trouble once—a question of place in line, booze-fueled threats, shoving. Vithu stepped forward and surprised everyone with a vicious chop to an ear that knocked the troublemaker down and drew blood from a gash on his scalp. The Boyz candidates quieted.

The sex was exciting, but not the way he thought it would be. Camaraderie was the high, the laughter and joy of his new friends, the ones he was pledging his life to.

When Vithu helped himself to the girl and spread his other hand next to her head, Samay saw HATE tattooed on those fingers. Vithu was a strange man.

No matter. This was the greatest night of Samay's young life.

Bauk was good.

Brotherhood was good.

****

Samay trudged through the muddy banks of the Saugus River, the crooked finger that poked the coastline just north of Boston before meandering through Ocean Park. He and Vithu waded through ragweed and cattails, each with a hand grasping chain links on the curving, rusted fence around North Shore Auto Salvage. Their feet plunged into sandy gray mud that sucked nosily and stank like something alive—or dead.

Samay scratched his arm. He'd been tattooed the night before, right after bauk, and the skin was irritated. A row of Khmer letters, whimsical curls and wavy lines, ran the length of his arm. Two of his three rites of initiation were complete—the Brotherhood of Bauk and the branding of the Khmer sign of the Asian Boyz. Only the Lesson was left.

Not that the Lesson was much. They were to retrieve guns because Pon said a war was coming. A simple, boring task, hardly worthy of the term Lesson. Samay was more anxious to learn the Asian Boyz trade—jacking cars and pulling B&Es. He'd been recruited because of his speed and athleticism, and he was anxious to prove himself.

"Maybe they're not here yet. We should go," Samay said, shaking his bothersome arm as if he could flick the ink off.

Vithu continued, pushing back a big swath of weeds with his free hand. Dusk approached, and if they timed this right, the day's last light would help them find what they were looking for and oncoming darkness would hide their leaving.

The tick of an outboard engine grew loud. They sank behind the growth. Samay's buttocks touched the ground and the moist soil wet his pants like a cold sponge. A skiff puttered by, captained by an old man wearing a knit cap. He navigated the shallow channel, weaving toward the Saugus marshes.

Vithu clapped the shoulder of his sore arm. "If Pon said they're here, then there's no doubt. None."

They continued on the cloying soil. The sun was almost down, streaks of yellow and red reflecting its last light. The temperature dropped so fast it felt as if they'd walked into a freezer.

Samay zippered his coat to the collar and thrust hands into pockets. Without the aid of the fence, he stepped awkwardly, bushwhacked by tall weeds Vithu let swing. "Pon," he said louder, stretching the name in a high voice. "Everyone talks of Pon. Everyone fears him. Why can't he carry his own guns? Is he afraid?"

Vithu cocked his head for an instant, but kept moving and answered.

"My friend, Pon is an avenging angel, and everything he does has meaning. When Buddha acts, Pon is his hand. You have been chosen. Feel fortunate. You ask if he is afraid? The only fear he knows is the one he brings."

Fortunate? For an arm that screams pain? A silly mission? And Vithu—he was different now that he'd recruited Samay and the initiation was almost over. Quiet. Serious. Samay looked at the old man in the boat, a speck in the distance, and wished he were riding with him. Maybe not, he thought. Rivers have ends, and right now he felt like traveling far. He glanced the other way to the open ocean.

"You made your choice," Vithu said. "Never regret it. And never disrespect Pon. His ears are everywhere."

Samay shuddered, not because he was cold, but because Vithu had just read his mind. *Coincidence?*

Samay's legs were still shaky from squatting, and he almost stumbled.

Near the corner of the junkyard fence, in the shadow of a rusting sandwich of Dodge Diplomat, Ford F-150, and a late model Sentra, three gray suitcases sat, handles up. Vithu flipped the hinges on one and let the top fall to the ground. Automatic pistols gleamed from cutouts in hard foam, out of place in the mudscape of the river bank. He snapped the suitcase shut and stood silently until the last light disappeared.

"See?" He nodded toward the last rays of the day. "Everything is as he said. Even the sun is commanded by Pon."

"So this is the Lesson?" Samay asked and shrugged, palms up.

Vithu hoisted the smallest suitcase, cradled it on his forearm, flipped the latches, opened the top. A pair of severed hands lay in a foam cutout, closed in tight fists, thumbs clenched around the first and second fingers. Flesh and bone had been cut clean at the wrists.

Vithu clutched Samay's tattooed arm and pulled him close. The hands looked fake, but Samay knew otherwise when he smelled an odor like uncooked steak. He tried to step back, his gorge rising.

Vithu's face was as tight as the fists, inches away from Samay's.

"He doubted Pon too, my friend. You've been given a second chance by our merciful leader. Witness the Lesson."

****

That same evening, Channary walked in a quiet, spacious courtyard. The American woman—Shee-la—held her hand in a warm, gentle grip. Strange. Shee-la was white but spoke Khmer perfectly. She walked straight and tall like a model, a woman of importance, but she treated Channary like a princess.

The courtyard was surrounded by flat-roofed buildings so high they blocked the sun and cast cool shadows. Porches lined each floor, their railings grinning like smiling teeth.

They came to a tall building, a great green box as big as a temple. An old Cambodian woman on the bottom landing wore a red sampot that touched her sandaled feet, a loose white blouse, and a krama scarf that hid her neck. Her long hair, parted in the middle, was pulled back tight like a working woman's.

"*Chhmua ei?*" the woman called, stretching the words.

"Channary," she answered.

Shee-la led her up the steps and into a house with hallways the color of rainbows. The familiar scent of incense greeted them, then the mouth-watering smell of meat cooking in oil. They passed a prayer room with a golden Buddha sitting on a table. A kitchen next, with more women, and Cambodian children and teenagers at tables, working and eating.

So this was America. *Different. But the same.*

They stopped at the end of the hall and the beginning of a narrow staircase. A bright round light shone from a ceiling high above and made the stairs and railing gleam.

Shee-la loosened her grip, kissed the top of Channary's head, and backed away. The Cambodian woman clasped Channary's hand in a grip that was hard, firm, and strong, and together they climbed the stairs.

Chapter 4

His wife's campaign headquarters reminded Conley of an after-prom party. Staffers, mostly kids, nailed posters of Lisa to the wall, slouched behind flimsy tables in folding chairs, and talked on phones in happy, sing-song voices.

He sat in a metal chair and waited near a picture window that framed the snarled traffic in City Hall Square. Car exhaust swelled from the cold and billowed like clouds that had fallen to earth. A pretty young blonde named Mandy kept smiling at him and asking if he wanted coffee. Three cups later, his face hurt from smiling back and the caffeine rush was making the hair on his arms tingle.

Lisa snuck up behind him and whispered, "Jail bait, Detective Conley."

His wife hugged him and he hugged back, smelling the lavender shampoo he'd bought her last Christmas.

"But she gives such great coffee," he said.

Lisa strode to her office, a jerry-built structure with temporary walls and a window to the busy staff area. He was close behind, drinking in the scent of good perfume and savoring the sight of his wife's magnificent glutes.

God bless Stairmaster machines.

She sank into the black leather office chair and he sat on the corner of the desk near the window. Her strawberry hair fanned the top of the chair, looking richer than the dark leather. She stretched her legs in front of him and he saw lean muscles tense. Lisa was Sicilian, blessed with mocha-colored skin. Her legs were as smooth as her campaign speech, with nary a freckle or blemish.

Mandy stuck her head in the open doorway. "More coffee Mr. Conley? Mrs. Conley?"

"We're good, Mandy. Matt's beautiful blue eyes are turning brown."

Mandy giggled and trotted back to her desk, blonde ponytail flashing.

Lisa picked up a rubber band and twirled it on her long index finger. "Mandy has a crush on you."

They laughed together. He couldn't remember the last time that happened. When the baby died, their marriage started to die too, and the memory of the infant struggling in its incubator became a recurring nightmare.

Brandon. He had a name—Brandon.

A name neither of them spoke during two years of emptiness and paralysis. But he still craved Lisa's presence, her touch, her voice, a primeval ache that never stopped. If only he could make her feel the same.

Today was their one-month separation anniversary. Other than quick, tense phone calls, the only time they communicated now was during their bizarre marriage counseling sessions with Dr. Larkin. The doctor was convinced marriage problems were caused by one-word virtues and vices, and finding the right ones was the key to fixing relationships. The word jumble was driving Conley crazy.

Sex, Dr. Larkin? That surely isn't the trouble with

our marriage. If anything, sex was the glue.

Money? No problem there either. Lisa's salary as an attorney and my detective pay bought us twin Beamers and a condo at the beach.

She put her hand over his and he felt electricity, and fantasized her saying, "Let's forget this bullshit, Matt. How about a nooner?"

"Lisa, there's something I've got to tell you about—"

"I heard about the murder in St. Amby's," she interrupted.

He nodded. "Two days ago. I need to give you a heads up about what happened. Eddie and I were called to investigate—"

"Your priest friend must be freaked."

"Father McCarrick acts like he's in charge, but I know when he's upset. Talks like he's high on helium. A guy named Victor Rodriguez was the vic, Puerto Rican with a big insurance business. Insured most of the Hispanics in Ocean Park."

She leaned forward, looked interested, concerned, caring, which made him think about…

Unselfishness. "Marriage is not all about you, Matt. Think about your wife."

"Congressman Conley," he said. "That has a ring to it, Lisa. Think you have a chance?"

She flattened her hands on the desk and hunched forward as if sharing a secret. "Special elections are always tough and I'm fighting an incumbent, but I'm polling in first place, Matt. Ahead of Congressman Diaz. Lots of rumors around his extracurricular activities. Nasty stuff. Kinky sex."

"Are they true?"

"I have no idea." She winked. "But my campaign manager—Bill McNulty—takes every opportunity to remind voters."

Ambition—that's certainly a candidate for the cause of our troubles. Lisa is married to me and a couple of careers—Essex County prosecutor and aspiring politician.

"If you got in, it'd be great for Ocean Park. You'd help turn it around."

She wrinkled her nose. "Bill says Marblehead and Swampscott are the key towns—places to build a political career. Do you remember Bill? You met at the District Attorney's Christmas party."

"I think so. Skinny guy, porn star mustache, wimpy handshake. Kind of a pretty boy."

Jealousy? Be careful. He imagined Larkin wagging his index finger and shaking his head in warning.

The corner of her mouth twitched and she squinted mischievously. "Bill and I don't shake hands and I haven't seen a lot of pornos, Matt, so I really can't compare. He's pretty trim, though."

"Lisa, let me tell you about that night in the church."

The hollow door to her office swung open. Bill McNulty strode in and threw Monday's *Ocean Park Gazette* on her desk. The paper scattered, tumbling as if he'd brought a windstorm. Lisa sat upright, hands folded, elbows planted on the edge of the desk.

McNulty spoke before she got a chance to.

"Disaster, Lisa. Potential fucking disaster."

Smiling didn't seem a natural reaction to that, but Lisa did it anyway. She smiled like a marionette—upturned mouth and dead eyes. "Bill, you remember

Matt."

His wife was practicing *Self-Control. Very good, Lisa. Wait, that was two words, couldn't be one of Dr. Larkin's babies. Did hyphenated words count?*

Conley stuck his hand out, determined to show…

Tolerance. Man, this is harder than I thought.

McNulty ignored the hand.

"Lisa, your husband is front page news," he said, slapping the desk. "The media loves this shit. You just gave Diaz the lead. Guaranteed."

"Bill, slow down. I haven't seen this." She flattened the paper with her hands and started to read.

McNulty snatched the front page from her and touched a different finger to his thumb for every phrase. "Well, let me be the first to inform you of the charges against Detective Conley. 'Detective Edward Jackson testified Conley was drinking on the job, used force recklessly, compromised a murder scene, destroyed church property, and endangered an eight-year-old child.' Your husband fucked up big time, and you'll pay for it by losing this election. Guilt by association." He jabbed his finger at her, inches away from her forehead. "That's how the public sees it. You just blew your lead."

Anger. Dr. Larkin always reminded them—anger bred anger. McNulty's was certainly stoking his.

Conley spoke quietly, evenly. "Don't talk to my wife like that."

Mandy stuck her head in the office door. "More coffee?"

"Not now, Mandy," Lisa called. "Close the door please, honey?"

"Look," McNulty continued, voice rising,

mustache dancing. "I don't need this shit, Lisa. I have other job offers if you're not going to control him."

Conley came around the desk and flattened his hand against McNulty's bony chest. "I said stop it. Now."

McNulty looked down and attempted to push the hand away. "This is actionable, Detective. It's called assault. You sure you want to add this to all the shit you're in?"

Lisa gently pulled his hand away. She turned and touched the newspaper with her fingertips.

"Matt, is this true? Did you do this?"

Trust. Bingo. Trust—or the lack of it, had hung like a sword over the relationship ever since they'd met. The five-letter monster needed to be conquered if the marriage was to survive.

And McNulty?—well, better face facts. Lisa wanted to be a politician. Better get used to her keeping company with assholes.

Assholes.

"No, Lisa, I didn't. Too bad you had to even ask."

Conley shrugged into his jacket and headed back through the bullpen of giggling staffers. He didn't answer his wife's plea to come back, or Mandy's happy goodbye as he stepped outside to the blast of honking horns sharpened by the cold crisp air.

Chapter 5

Conley sat between the two priests. Father Spinelli leaned toward Captain Stefanos, elbows sliding on the scarred conference table. Spinelli turned the back of his head to the others so no one would hear, and whispered, "Captain, we'll need a copy of the police report—for the insurance company."

Father McCarrick heard, leaned toward his fellow priest and said, "Want him to sign it in blood, Frank?"

Stefanos sighed, shuffling pages into a folder until they were as neat and aligned as everything on his person—a tie knot so perfect it looked like a clip-on, white shirt stretched across broad chest without a wrinkle, gray hair cropped like a drill instructor.

He glanced toward the door.

"Fathers, we'll get you a copy of the report by Friday. The social worker's waiting. Now remember," he said, index finger raised, serious brown eyes threatening each priest in turn, "the crying statue is our secret. If the press finds out, they'll turn the church into a circus."

Conley took notes.

Crying statue equals circus.

Stefanos, Conley's new special assignment boss with the Massachusetts State Police, hadn't discussed that with him. In fact, the state police captain forgot to do a lot of things—like invite Conley to the morning meetings. The list of surprise notes was growing. They needed to talk.

The captain's assistant sat across from him. Detective Lloyd Kendricks was black, as well-dressed as Stefanos, with bigger shoulders and a thicker middle. He had mismatched eyes—one brown, the other a disturbing cloudy cue ball whose color matched the light in the Bluetooth he wore.

The priests scraped back their chairs on the green speckled tiles. They'd spent the past hour bickering in the windowless room at Ocean Park Police headquarters, questioning Stefanos more than he questioned them. Now Fathers McCarrick and Spinelli eyed each other like prizefighters, jockeyed to see who would be first out of the police conference room, and almost knocked into the woman and girl in the doorway.

The young girl from the church—Channary— walked in. She surveyed the room, perhaps checking the contrasting shades of green above and below the chair rail. The light on the silver video camera in the corner blinked—green, of course.

"Channary," Stefanos said, bending at the waist and shaking her hand. "You have a beautiful name, Channary. Welcome."

He didn't seem like a bad guy, but he was out of his league. A Marine buzz-cut and broad shoulders might impress people in Boston or Worcester, but it didn't buy much in a place like Ocean Park. O-P ran on relationships and favors and tribal knowledge. The skin tags were the real power brokers, informants who got their nickname from the local cops. Ugly, useless appendages on humanity—skin tags—low-level pushers and punks who greased their businesses by selling information.

In Ocean Park you just knew—*knew* that when a lot of Outlaws rode their Harleys around Dom's Lounge, a major drug deal was going down.

Knew that when the boosters jacked stereos and handbags from cars in the Walmart parking lot, they fenced the stuff at jewelry and pawn shops on Monroe Street.

Knew that the hookers in City Hall Square used local cabs to conduct business, and always paid the hack drivers in trade.

That's how Ocean Park worked and it took years to learn the people and places. And the big black guy, Stefano's quiet, sinister-looking assistant? He wasn't going to help much either because quiet and shy didn't work at all in O-P, no matter how bad you looked.

Stefanos led the girl to a chair, produced lollipops from the pocket of his jacket, and spread them in front of her. She looked scared as a jackrabbit. She folded her arms and lowered her chin to her chest.

The woman introduced herself as Sheila Thompson from Health and Human Services. Black Irish. Coal-colored hair and skin that looked like porcelain. A bit on the skinny side. She wore a gray pinstripe suit that might have made her look mannish if not for the gold triangle earrings that accentuated her long, slender neck.

"Captain Stefanos," she said, all business, "Channary's been through a lot. She's blocking the memory of that night in church."

"We need to try, Ms. Thompson."

Channary's eyes flickered to Stefanos, then to

Conley.

"Sheila," the captain said, "ask Channary why she was in church so late."

Thompson spoke in Khmer, graceful throat working, lips and tongue dancing, and the little girl's eyes grew. Channary answered. Thompson translated.

"Channary says it's always good to be in a church."

"Who else was there?" Stefanos asked.

More Cambodian, back and forth. Channary pointed to Conley.

"Did she come to the church with Mr. Rodriguez?" Stefanos asked.

Channary nodded.

"What was her relationship—no, ask if she saw anyone other than Conley and Victor Rodriguez?"

Channary listened and suddenly rattled off a burst of Cambodian with such melodious inflections that her sentences sounded like songs.

Thompson paused a few seconds. "She's talking about the statues, but she doesn't know their names. The old man with the beard and book, the long-haired man standing on a serpent."

An intense hour later, not much had been learned. Channary spoke earnestly, seeking approval after every answer. Thompson hesitated.

"Captain, we're concerned Channary may be a victim of sex trafficking. Friends International in Cambodia is helping us track her family. The country's infamous for orphan tourists, predators who pretend to help, but prey on the most vulnerable." She smoothed the girl's hair and continued, "I'll stick with her, see what I can find out. I placed her with some Cambodian families on River Street for the time being. I'll teach her some English and—"

"No," Stefanos said.

"Oh?" One equally graceful eyebrow arched. "Why not?"

He leaned forward, poised to intimidate, and his face hardened. "Place her in a normal foster home. The Asian Boyz and the Latin Kings are fighting over the city's drug trade. River Street's a battleground. It's unsafe. I won't allow it. Put her in a normal foster situation."

Thompson shot back. "Channary's an abandoned eight-year-old who doesn't speak our language, Captain. Try finding foster parents who speak Khmer. Besides, the Cambodian ladies will keep her safe. Health and Human Services is making this call. Case closed."

Conley smiled. Sheila Thompson was a warrior. Kendricks turned and leveled that smoky malamute eye on him, just before touching his hand to his Bluetooth.

"Captain, we got another customer."

"Where?"

"The beach."

Stefanos gathered the folders from the table, threw them into his briefcase, and strode out of the room with Kendricks. With a roll of his eyes, Conley followed, past conference rooms, the front desk, and onto the concrete steps. Stefanos stood at the bottom as Kendricks retrieved their car. Stefanos turned and placed his open hand on Conley's chest. Thick fingers. Calloused palm. Immovable arm.

"Detective, why don't you sit this one out? Get a copy of the report to the priests."

Conley fought his own urge to raise an eyebrow. "I can do that later, Captain."

Kendricks braked to a stop in front of them and rolled the window down.

Stefanos' gaze lifted from Conley's knees to the general area of his face. "Tell you the truth, son, I don't care if you do it now, later, or never. I said sit this one out."

"Captain, you could really use my help. Is there a problem?"

Kendricks called from the driver's seat. "Let me take this one, sir. Half of Ocean Park's finest are known to be on gang payrolls, and you, Detective Conley, even topped that. You drank on duty, discharged a firearm for no good reason, and are a generally useless piece of dung. How's that for a 'problem'?" He turned to Stefanos. "Did I cover everything, Captain?"

"The liquor wasn't mine," Conley said

"Jackson says it was," Kendricks shot back. "Also says you fired the gun, that's why you had it when we showed up."

"My pal Eddie would blame the Pope if he thought it would protect his pension. Captain, I wasn't drinking and I didn't fire in the church. The internal investigation will prove that."

"Okay."

"I can help you."

"I can't afford to deal with the Ocean Park force. The D.A. says they have a bribery problem."

"But I've done nothing wrong."

"Why'd you have your partner's gun? You're either guilty or stupid, Conley. Take your pick."

"Maybe they was sharing a pint, Captain,"

Kendricks said. "Then he'd be only half to blame."

"Conley, you're a question mark," Stefanos said. "You bring nothing to the table."

He headed for the car. Conley followed.

"Captain, you're making a mistake. I can help. I'm asking you to reconsider."

You need me.

Stefanos stopped and faced him. "I said no. Don't take it personally, Detective. It's just business. Maybe next time."

Something behind Conley caught Stefanos' eye. Conley turned to see Sheila Thompson and Channary at the top of the stairs. Beside him Stefanos eyed Thompson for three long seconds, then smiled at Channary as they descended the steps to cross the street. By the time Conley looked back at Stefanos, the captain had the car door open and was sliding inside.

Before he closed the door, Conley heard him mutter to Kendricks, "Damned if I'm going to lose two pissing contests today, Lloyd."

****

Less than an hour later, Conley watched Stefanos and Kendricks leave the crime scene, then called to the tech still working it. The tech was dressed in a HAZMAT suit, waist-deep in a Dumpster behind the roast beef stand across from the beach. The body of a young Hispanic lay on the pile of garbage inside the green container.

"Tommy 'the Dog' Lopez," Conley said. "King of the Ocean Park drug trade."

The tech nodded and pointed at the bloody stumps where the corpse's hands had been severed at the wrists. "No hands."

"They're probably still dealing coke down on Union Street."

"Or at the high school maybe."

"Or the junior high."

The tech moved like an astronaut in his bulky gear. He lifted his leg, straddled Tommy Lopez, and inspected the twisted neck, flesh bunched like a wrung towel. The movement stirred the trash, piles of grease-stained paper bags, burnt French fries, rancid meat. Bottle flies buzzed, swarmed away, boomeranged back.

"Two Hispanics in a week," the tech said.

"Not sure that means anything. They lived at opposite ends of the 'Rican solar system. One would think Tommy had a lot more opportunities to piss people off than Victor Rodriguez."

"One would think."

"'Course Mr. Rodriguez might have said the business world ain't always nice either."

"What about gangs?"

"Tommy was involved for sure. A major player," Conley said and pocketed his notebook. "I'll check it out."

Chapter 6

Later that afternoon, Conley climbed the peeling stairs to the front porch of a big colonial. An army of garden gnomes defended Simon O'Neil's front lawn. The ceramic soldiers guarded birdbaths, gazing balls, wooden geese with windmill wings, plywood cutouts of bent-over, fat-assed ladies gardening. Wind socks and chimes crammed the space between rail and roof, a flapping, clanging curtain. He caught a splinter on the wooden rail and stopped to inspect his hand.

A shrill voice called from the door. "You here for the cats?"

A woman with a startling shock of white hair and a wrinkled face stood behind the screen. A faded pink housedress draped her skinny frame.

"Pardon?" he said.

"You gotta have a net or something." She punched a fist in the air. "Tools. BB-guns."

He flashed his badge.

"I'm Matt Conley, Mrs. O'Neil. Remember me? I went to school with your son William."

Another crop of white hair appeared behind her, this one shorter. Simon O'Neil.

"Gracie, that's the Conley boy. Billy's friend, don't you remember?"

O'Neil eased his confused wife back into the darkness and returned, opened the screen door, and waved Conley in.

"Matt, please come in. Of course we remember you."

Simon O'Neil adjusted his glasses—big, square-framed jobs that magnified his tired brown eyes. Conley edged by, the smells of cabbage and Mr. O'Neil's stale, moth-bitten sweater joining to greet him. Mrs. O'Neil sat in a rocking chair and studied Conley with slatted eyes.

O'Neil turned the television on for his wife.

"He gonna catch those damn cats?" she asked urgently, head thrust forward, skinny rump perched precariously on the edge of the chair.

"Stay there, Gracie," her husband answered with a wag of his finger.

He was glad Mr. O'Neil used the word "there". She might not have given a care to be commanded like a dog, but Conley had long been conditioned to shoulder the misfortune of others. Irish Catholics liked to savor guilt in all its delicious forms.

O'Neil led him through the ancient kitchen. White appliances looked diseased, pocked with black spots showing through chipped paint. Yellowed wallpaper repeated a pattern of a horse-drawn carriage traveling under lush oaks—about five hundred times. Blue linoleum had been worn away in front of the sink and stove to reveal rough subfloor.

He followed Simon O'Neil, and when squeaky hinges closed the back door behind them, they stood in a yard of colossal neglect. Conley had been there years ago with William, when the two of them stole his father's wine grapes from the vines. Mr. O'Neil caught them and they swore innocence, lying vehemently through purple lips plastered with grape skins.

Bushes and small trees were winter bare, their brown, rotting leaves piled like fat aprons around roots. The lawn was a checkerboard of dirt spots and long clumps of straw-colored grass. Rusted metal tools lay in random places.

O'Neil led him to a structure used to support grapevines. The rickety wooden arbor was gray with age, and bare, withered vines snaked through the trellis, a tangle of brittle brown thatch. The old man invited him to sit on a low stone bench covered with mold and moss, the only things that seemed to flourish in the yard.

"Grace is suffering from dementia," he said. "She sees cats everywhere. Thanks for coming, Matt. I was worried no one would care about my complaint."

"You were expecting me?"

He put his hands under his haunches. "Matt, I complained to the police about that colored cop. Didn't they tell you? Isn't that why you came?"

Kendricks.

Kendricks must have already been there, surely because of Father McCarrick's deposition about the old chicken-blood-on-the-statue prank. Conley hesitated, weighing the benefits of lying against the difficulty of what he needed to accomplish.

"Yes," he lied, removing notepad and pen from his inside pocket. "Headquarters sent me, Mr. O'Neil."

"Good. I was afraid they'd think I was a nuisance."

"No, sir. We are public servants, after all."

O'Neil smiled, revealing black and yellow teeth fighting for space.

"That eye, Matt. The monstrous blue eye that

colored boy had. You know what that means, don't you?"

"Birth defect?"

O'Neil grunted. "No, son. I thought you were smarter than that. One brown eye, one blue means his mother was white. He's an abomination, no mistaking it." O'Neil pronounced abomination phonetically, as if he'd just invented the word.

Conley changed the subject.

"Mr. O'Neil, how's William these days?"

"He's very well. Working hard. You should get together. He always talks about the time you two fought those bullies in the park."

Conley had almost forgotten. He and William had been altar boys at St. Ambrose's. William was really into the Church and seemed to be heading for priesthood. He was more principled than other kids his age, and the only time he seemed to get into trouble was when Conley led him there.

"Damn police here bothering me with silly questions while the devil's recruits are handing out dope needles and marijuana sticks like candy."

Conley opened his notebook. He didn't really need to record anything. His goal was to capture a nugget of information, something Kendricks and Stefanos didn't know about the murder of Victor Rodriguez, leverage to get back on the case. Probably a long shot given the bizarre nature of the visit so far.

He wrote O'Neil in the notebook and surrounded the name with flowing brackets, wavy, curving molding. He doodled as O'Neil talked—drew a spiral so tight it almost sprang from the page, along with pyramids, squares, rectangles that became castles when he added crenellations.

"Ocean Park's going to hell," O'Neil said and told him all the reasons why.

Conley found he'd drawn two squares next to each other and connected the tops so they looked like O'Neil's eyeglasses. He filled the squares with big eyes, careful to capture the dilated pupils, and was so absorbed in his artwork he didn't realize O'Neil had stopped talking.

"Matt," O'Neil said, his face inches away, a real life doodle of eyeglasses, gray stubble, and nose covered with thin red veins, "are you getting all this?"

Those damn milky glasses were spooky. Now Conley knew what fish in aquariums felt like.

"Yessir," he said, hugging notebook to chest and sliding back on the rough seat.

"Why didn't the colored policeman ask me about Mr. Rodriguez?"

"You knew Victor Rodriguez?"

"Of course I did. For many years. He hired William."

The bench under Conley felt colder all of a sudden. The sky over the park stilled, and nature seemed to pause for a discovery.

"Mr. O'Neil, does William sell insurance for Victor Rodriguez?"

O'Neil smiled, a ghastly mask. "No, Matt, he's a manager, a very good one. Victor Rodriguez owned a restaurant downtown. Morgan's Tap."

Calling Morgan's Tap a restaurant was like calling hell a warm weather destination. Restaurant? Maybe if you called a big jar of pig's feet in brine on the bar pub fare. Microwave pizza?—European cuisine.

Morgan's was the toughest bar in the city, maybe on the whole North Shore. The idea of Morgan's being "managed" was absurd, akin to saying prison riots or cattle stampedes had oversight and organization.

"Mr. O'Neil, are you sure Victor Rodriguez owned the Tap?"

"Of course he did. Put William in charge some time ago. They came by here occasionally and Mr. Rodriguez always made it a point to tell me what a gem our William is."

Time to talk with his old friend William, the unlikely gem of a manager of a crazy house fueled with grimy shelves of cheap booze and draft beer. Conley wasn't sure he'd even recognize William, but he was sure he dreaded visiting Morgan's Tap. No sane person strolled into the place alone, and even Ocean Park cops weren't allowed to enter without backup.

He stood. Simon O'Neil looked up at him, and when he grasped Conley's forearm, the old man's skin felt like paper that would tear and blow away in a strong wind. His voice got louder but not stronger.

"Matt, where are you going? We have more to talk about."

The hinges to the back door creaked and Mrs. O'Neil appeared, a butcher knife in each hand. Her robe was missing, one strap of her nightgown had fallen, and a white pancake breast quivered behind her upraised arms.

"Grace," Mr. O'Neil called as he scrambled from the bench, traipsed the path of long grass to his wife and repeated her name, chanting it as if pleading for divine assistance.

Calling out a farewell, Conley took the opportunity

to leave and found a path beside the house that led him past a handsome family of plastic deer grazing on the shriveled remains of last summer's ragweed.

****

Simon O'Neil's house was receding in his rearview mirror when Lisa called.

"Matt, I've been trying to reach you for days."

"I've been pretty busy."

"I'm sorry for what I said the other day."

"So am I."

"I spoke to Father McCarrick. He told me you're leading the Rodriguez investigation. Shows you what I know. I'm very proud of you."

"He said that, huh?"

Long silence before she spoke again. "When are you coming by?"

He stopped at the light on Chestnut Street. A canopy of oaks spread over him, and he was losing reception. Lisa's voice was garbled. "Love" snuck through before static. The word "babe" made its way out of the crackle.

The sound finally cleared. "When, Matt?"

"Soon." The light turned green. "Very soon."

Chapter 7

The crowd was a gathering of impressive proportions, maybe the largest in Ocean Park history. White, black, Hispanic, Asian, all were in attendance for the political event of the year—a fundraiser for Congressman Hector Diaz's re-election. Samay stayed as close to Diaz as he inconspicuously could as the politician waded into a sea of constituents. Diaz hugged a fat old woman who wore eye-watering perfume. Her husband was next—fragrant stale breath and a hint of Ben Gay. Handshake followed with a middle-aged man with large, calloused hands and beer breath. Young woman with good cleavage next. The baby in her arm, a chubby infant who smelled of milk and talcum powder and dirty diaper, squirmed as if to defend his mother's breasts.

The Hispanic Social Club, the largest hall in Ocean Park, was the unofficial headquarters of the Latin Kings gang. On this Friday night the club was the venue for one of Diaz's campaign speeches, and its doors were open to every prospective voter in the city—including Asian Boyz. The congressman brushed past the long, elegant drapes alongside the tall windows, looked at his reflection in a wall mirror, and adjusted his red tie and pocket hankie. His pencil mustache danced when he smiled.

He crossed the hall, shaking hands, hugging, and

complimenting everyone in his path. Heavy girl with a tight dress. Boy in a wheelchair. A rabbi. A nun. The politician swiveled from one vote to another as he made his way through the kitchen to the small club bar. Diaz left happy people behind, still talking about the speech he'd given, the promise of jobs, tax cuts that would somehow coexist with more services, and the silly drivel about progress that his opponent, Lisa Conley, was preaching. Everyone laughed with him.

Samay and Vithu followed into the crowded bar. The clack of pool balls interrupted the drone of a hockey game on the high television. The club bar was a place where gangbangers mingled with upright club members like Congressman Diaz.

Ramon, the Social Club manager, joined Diaz at a table along with a red-faced cop named Madigan. Ramon's long hair and eyelashes would have made him look effeminate if not for his five-o'clock shadow, square jaw, and dark goatee.

A waitress brought them a bottle of tequila and glasses. Samay and Vithu found cue sticks and racked the balls at the pool table next to them. Diaz and his companions spoke softly, too softly to overhear in the crowded space—until they opened their second bottle.

"Tommy Lopez is dead," Ramon said. "Someone fucked him up real bad."

Break. Three-ball dropped in the corner pocket. Samay positioned himself with his back to them and pretended to study his next shot.

"Life's not for everyone," Diaz said. "Who killed him?"

"Fuck if I know," the policeman said.

"We need to know." Diaz poured himself a drink.

Vithu finally made a shot and contemplated his options. Samay circled slowly until he could see Diaz's table.

Madigan reached into the pocket of his jacket and produced a packet of paper. He unfolded it slowly, slid the creased page across the table, and lifted his hand from a photo nestled inside. A young girl's face was blurred but angelic, tilted upward to a dark-haired woman as they descended the steps from the Ocean Park police station, past two white cops and a black one. Samay recognized the girl from the River Street courtyard.

Diaz inspected the photo before he drained the rest of his drink.

"She knows who killed Victor," the cop said. "She was there. Cambodian."

"Cambodians," Ramon said. "Cockroaches. What stinks more, the foul river they live near or their filthy tenements?"

"Why haven't you made an arrest?" Diaz demanded.

Madigan shrugged. "State Police took over the investigation, and they ain't sharing names."

"Then ask her," Diaz ordered Ramon and tapped the picture twice, fast, as if his fingertip would burn if left there too long.

"What?"

"Ask the girl."

Diaz crumpled the paper into a ball, crushing it ever smaller with manicured fingers.

Ramon, still looking stunned, said, "I can use Tommy's gang, but I'll need a translator."

Diaz nodded, then steepled his hands under his

43

chin and issued a command to Madigan.

"Don't respond to 911 calls on River Street. Keep your people away."

****

"Now?" Samay whispered hours later.

"It's time," Vithu said.

They opened the closet door from the inside and stepped into the dark, quiet Hispanic Club kitchen. Samay retrieved the pipe cutter from his baggy pant leg. Dim moonlight poured in through the six-pane windows. Vithu flicked the light switch on and Samay climbed onto the wide industrial stove and braced himself across its hood. Legs dangling, arms and torso wedged between steel and wall, he fit the open jaw of the cutter on the copper gas pipe. Steel or black iron would have been difficult, but the tool cut through the copper after ten turns, and natural gas hissed. He righted himself. Vithu collected wet rags from the bar and wadded them under the doors to the bar and hall. The steady hiss of gas filled the room, along with a stink like sulfur. They closed the kitchen door, stepped into the dark hall, and paced the thirty-seven steps they'd counted earlier when they walked behind Diaz.

The deadbolt on the side door slid easily, as did the two high-quality Schlage locks. They stepped into the parking lot and eased the metal door closed behind them.

Vithu paused, turning to admire the impressive two-story building with stylish awnings over doors and windows. He ran a hand over the wall.

"Pon says the war begins today," he whispered to the bricks. "Say goodbye to your castle, Hector."

The moon was a bright coin, but dark factories and

44

close tenements gave cover as they ran. Blocks later, they climbed the steep berm to the railroad tracks for the commuter train to Boston. Their legs pistoned the hill and a small avalanche of soil and coal tumbled down.

Vithu reached the top and slid his new SIG Sauer out of his holster. He planted the handle of the gun on the back of his left hand, pointing the barrel at the square target of light in the kitchen they'd just left. He squeezed the trigger and a fireball bloomed from the Hispanic Social Club. Windows shattered, car alarms crowed. He pulled Samay to the worn walking path between the rails and the fireball grew as they raced toward the river.

Chapter 8

Dares, death wishes, and drunkenness brought normal people to Morgan's Tap. Conley had visited twice years ago—a combination of dare and drunkenness called him and his college buddies.

He cruised past the bar on Saturday afternoon and parked across the street. An overhead railroad bridge and a brick warehouse cast a shadow on Morgan's for most of the day. Though bridge and building appeared responsible for the perpetual darkness, it seemed more likely God had decided not to waste His sunshine on Morgan's Tap.

A pit bull rooted in the gutter out front, stopping and sniffing energetically when it found something interesting. A bum wrapped in dirty blankets slept peacefully on the sidewalk under the bridge, prayer-ready hands providing a pillow like a sleeping child's.

The bar wore a façade of broken and faded bamboo slats. Conley opened the windowless door, and loose slats waved a greeting and chattered ominously when the door slammed shut.

Three people were in Morgan's—bartender sitting on a silver beer chest, studying the television on the wall—old guy leaning forward on a stool and sleeping on the bar, spill of long black hair over folded arms—platinum blonde working a video game with both hands, thin muscles visible under the narrow straps of her halter top.

Conley rested his forearms on the bar. The bartender slid off the beer chest and raised his chin in question.

"William O'Neil around?" Conley asked.

"Nope."

"Know where he is?"

"Ain't none of my business."

"Think he'll be back soon?"

"That ain't my business neither."

The girl at the game turned her head, but managed to keep the rest of her body focused on the game.

"How about a drink?" Conley asked. "That your business?"

The barkeep held out his hands, palms up.

Conley studied the gaudy plastic beer tap handles, surveyed the shelves of hard liquor on the wall, and said, "Club soda. No lime."

The bartender's face reddened. He plucked a glass out of the plastic rack in front of him, scooped ice out of a bucket, and shot squirts from a chrome soda gun into the glass like he was banging nails.

Conley felt warm flesh against his arm and turned. The blonde's arm was pressed tight.

She nodded sideways at him as she addressed the bartender. "Bill collector or salesman, Teddy? What do you think?"

"Donna, I ain't got a guess about this asshole," he said, and then, "salesman, maybe."

"Smart guess," Conley said, raising his glass in salute. "We're all selling something."

Teddy's eyebrows furrowed, actually sliding toward each other before the right one climbed high.

"I ain't a fucking salesman," he said.

Conley took a long drink. "You certainly aren't, Ted. Don't mind my bullshit. That's just the club soda talking."

Donna barked a loud "Hah!" and smiled wide enough to wrinkle her makeup. Teddy even grinned, figuring he'd won.

Conley glanced at the door. Clever repartee with barflies wasn't going to help find William O'Neil. He considered leaving and weighed it against waiting it out with a relatively tame crowd here at Chaos Central.

The hair at the end of the bar stirred like a mass of floating seaweed.

"What's so funny?" Seaweed Head asked, sleepy eyes still closed.

Donna's voice dropped an octave. "Maybe the handsome salesman here grabbed my ass and it felt pretty good, Rocco. Maybe it made me laugh, okay?"

Rocco lifted his head and stared through swollen eyelids and greasy bangs.

"Go back to sleep, honey," Donna said. "I'll wake you when I'm ready to go." She bumped Conley with her arm again. Fast friends already. "Unless, of course, I get a better offer."

Rocco slid off the stool and swayed dangerously before he steadied. He was wiry, barely over five feet, and unless there was a suicide bomb vest under his ratty sweatshirt, he was probably the least dangerous person to ever pass through Morgan's bamboo portal.

Donna laughed again. A faint rumble sounded outside.

Teddy poured Rocco a beer and set it on the bar. "Cool down, Rocco. Here. On the house."

"Don't want your beer, Teddy." He shoved the mug and it slid off the back of the bar top and crashed on the floor.

Conley finished his drink and stood. *Time to go.*

The outside rumble grew louder, building like the beginning of a thunderstorm.

Donna clutched his forearm with both hands and swung toward him, along with the tart smells of fresh beer and body odor. "Where you going, honey? Don't mind Rocco, he don't bite. Hell, he hardly got any teeth."

Thunder had come to ground and decided to visit Morgan's Tap. Conley looked through the window and saw at least a dozen Harleys, angled to the curb, throaty motors dying one by one.

Bikers poured into the Tap, giant hairy Vikings.

Rocco ran to the biggest one, turned, and pointed a dirty, accusing fingernail at Conley. His skinny hand was shaking, and when he spoke he sounded hysterical.

"Tony, that creep goosed Donna."

Rocco found some courage and spent it on a lazy roundhouse that Conley blocked with his forearm. But he didn't block the grubby underside of Tony's hammering fist, and fell to the floor, kissing the edge of the bar on the way. He scrambled to his feet, glanced at the door, but that path was blocked by an army in denim and leather. Conley turned to Teddy, considered flashing his badge, decided not to.

"Call 9-1-1," he said, and tasted the coppery tang of his own blood.

Teddy turned his palms up once more and smiled.

A fist rapped the back of Conley's head and he visited the floor again. Vision blurring, he crawled through a gauntlet of buckled black boots that stomped shoulders, back, legs. Suddenly the front door opened and shiny brown shoes appeared, a sight as improbable as a sunbeam. The mob parted. No one spoke. Heavy boots shuffled backward. The newcomer bunched Conley's jacket in the middle of his back and lifted him as easily as a lion lifting a cub. He passed his free hand over Conley's hanging, bleeding head, no doubt finalizing the baptism he had just received.

"Rocco, Tony, all of you," his savior said in a voice as deep and final as a grave, "touch my friend Matt again and I'll kill you."

Chapter 9

Minutes later Conley was being ministered to by the most beautiful black girl he'd ever seen. She studied gashes on his forehead and cheek, fat lips, crooked nose, then got to work. She worked intently, warm breath washing his face as she touched him on either side of the cuts and gently pulled skin apart.

William O'Neil sat in a straight chair behind her.

"Hello, Matt. Good to see you."

"You, too," he tried to say, but it came out "Yoo shoo". He was surprised how many places could hurt just from talking.

"Sorry the boys roughed you up. Things always seem to get out of control when Sage and I go out for lunch. I wish you'd called first. Sage will fix you up. She's a doctor."

Of course. And Teddy was a lawyer, Donna a diplomat, Rocco a CPA. Morgan's Tap was a regular hangout for Ocean Park's upper crust.

The woman retrieved a medical kit from a closet and removed alcohol, gauze, and bandages. She looked back at Conley and turned to the case for more supplies.

The office was neat and clean. The leather couch looked new and wood floors gleamed. An executive desk stood in back of them. Evidently, being CEO of Morgan's Tap had fringe benefits beyond scaring the hell out of bikers and hanging with beautiful doctors.

A picture frame displayed a gold USMC buckle behind glass. More frames held photos of William with men in fatigues—in a jungle, on a palm-treed beach, perched on the crag of a rocky hill that looked like a moonscape.

The woman—Sage—soaked pads in alcohol and swabbed his cuts as Conley watched it all in the mirror of her eyes. The reflection of her mocha-colored hands disappeared in her irises because they were the same color. The white gauze squares appeared to be dressing wounds by themselves.

William was no longer frail and certainly not small. Six-five maybe. Gangly but solid. His arms were so wide that when he straightened them, hands on knees, they looked like broadswords at rest.

Teddy brought two tall drinks, muddy and frothy, and placed them on the small table.

"Irish Car Bombs," William said with a smile. "What better drinks for two Micks to toast their reunion?"

"Sorry, William, but I didn't come here on a social call. I'm a policeman now."

"Figures. Some people are put on this world to screw it up and others are here to fix the screw-ups. You were always a fixer, Matt."

"I need to ask you about your boss. Victor Rodriguez."

He nodded.

"And where the hell you've been all these years," Conley said.

William took a long swig and folded his long arm-swords across his chest. "I'll start there. Makes more sense that way."

****

William O'Neil joined the military after high school, had a taste of battle, learned he was good at it. So good that private opportunity followed, a high-paid job chasing people good at screwing up the world. He'd also become a storyteller, and rendered his adventures more like a journalist than a mercenary.

Tears fell from the canopy in the Somali jungle, hot condensation that turned the jungle floor into a steaming cauldron. Monkeys chattered and beautiful birds cawed at the endless shower. Mud-hut villages outside Kandahar were cold and quiet—no noisy animals there, just listless, desperate people waiting to die. Winds in the desolate Peshawar mountains howled, blew relentlessly, angry and cruel, the only thing alive.

His strong jaw twitched, a tic Conley suddenly remembered. It was less pronounced now, barely perceptible.

"I'm back, Matt. Came home three months ago and heard Victor Rodriguez was looking for someone to run the Tap."

"Interesting job."

"And not many applicants. I had the inside track. He and my dad were friends."

"Two unlikely companions."

"Knew each other from St. Amby's. Holy Name Society."

"Really? Rodriguez was a parishioner?"

"A very dedicated member of the Church of St. Ambrose."

"Any idea who murdered him?"

"No, but I know who does. The Paladin."

"Who's he?"

"Paladin's a place—a social club."

"You mean like the Elks or the Hibernians?" Conley asked.

William took another long slug from his drink and wore a brown mustache before his tongue wiped it away.

"No. More social."

"I don't get it."

Sage glanced at William. He took a deep breath into his long, wide torso.

"Kinky stuff, Matt. You try my wife and I'll try yours."

Tic.

Sage pulled stitches through his eyebrow, hands moving so fast they fluttered. Conley was embarrassed that she had to hear this, hoped she was too occupied to be listening.

"William, Victor Rodriguez was a married man. He took his wife to sex parties?"

Tic.

"He took me," Sage said. She'd spoken for the first time, in a confident, detached voice that didn't interfere with her handiwork. "Victor took me to those parties."

Silence filled the room. Stunned, Conley avoided eye contact and took a deep breath. When he finally spoke, his words rasped from a parched throat.

"So you think the people at this club killed him?"

"They threatened to kill him," she said, drawing a stitch.

"Why?"

"I don't know."

"I need to find out."

"I'll help," William said.

Conley hesitated. *Not so fast.* The adult William may have been built like a steamroller and capable of scaring an entire biker gang, but he was a civilian. Conley's job status was tenuous enough without enlisting amateur sleuths.

"Thank you," Conley said, "but no."

"Matt, you need us. Without our help, you'll never find the Paladin."

Sage stopped working and turned to William, one eyebrow raised, and said "Our help?"

He nodded once, looking Conley directly in the eye. "Victor was our friend. We need to set this right. Sage and I want to be fixers too."

Chapter 10

One week after Victor Rodriguez's murder, Conley pulled into the rectory driveway and parked behind Father McCarrick's Buick. Mrs. Blodgett was already at the door. Somehow she seemed to know when visitors were coming.

"Prescient," McCarrick always said about his loyal housekeeper, proud that he'd found a word that made him sound smart and his housekeeper appear gifted. He'd even spell the word.

"Father, she's nosey," Conley always corrected. "N-O-S-E-Y."

She held the door open and her eyes brightened when she saw his damaged face.

"Matt, what in God's name happened to you?"

"When you fight crime, Mrs. Blodgett, sometimes crime fights back."

He walked past her into the rectory, into the Sunday-afternoon smell of a roast in the oven.

Father McCarrick sat at the dining room table reading the Catholic newspaper *The Pilot*, his finger running down the list of morally objectionable movies.

"Where's Father Francesco?" Conley asked.

"Boston. He and the Cardinal are busy counting pieces of silver. Who beat you up?"

"Bikers at Morgan's Tap."

Father grunted. "Morgan's. Only thing missing in

that place is brimstone."

"Father," Conley said, sliding into a chair and folding his hands on the linen tablecloth. McCarrick looked at him over the top of his reading glasses. "Victor Rodriguez. He was a parishioner, wasn't he?"

"What's this all about?"

"Just part of the investigation. Captain Stefanos never asked you that question. Rodriguez belonged to St. Ambrose parish."

"Yes. He did." Back to the newspaper.

"Why didn't you tell us that?"

"Don't offer anything you're not asked. Isn't that what they tell defendants, Matt? Yes or no answers?"

"Father, you're a material witness, not a defendant. You can say anything you think is relevant to solving the case."

"Fine. I found it irrelevant. Happy? I'm not a blabbermouth, you know."

McCarrick turned pages until he found *The Pilot's* morally objectionable book list and put his finger back to work.

"So, he must have come to confession here," Conley said.

Mrs. Blodgett pushed through the swinging door from the kitchen and placed a cup of tea in front of Father as he answered.

"Yes, he came to confession here. So what?"

The housekeeper laid the spoon next to the teacup, then decided it looked better on the other side. She cupped one hand near the edge of the table and used the other to meticulously sweep the clean tablecloth. Conley waited for her to finish. And waited. Finally, she left.

Asking Father to break a sacred vow would be an awful thing—reprehensible—unethical—downright immoral.

"Tell me what he confessed."

"Matt!"

"Sorry, but I thought we were playing the 'don't ask, don't tell' game."

"You damn well know I can't divulge what's said in the confessional."

"That didn't seem the case last New Year's Eve, Father. Lisa and I heard you tell everyone about Mrs. O'Donnell's adventures at the church party."

"I did not."

"You probably don't remember. Let's just hope Father Francesco doesn't find out."

McCarrick looked over the top of his newspaper.

"Is that blackmail or extortion, Matt? I get the two confused. Of course, I do remember a confession from a young man who had a stash of nudie books he stole from the pharmacy"—he jerked his thumb toward the window—"the one right across the street."

"That was a very long time ago. Tell anyone you want."

He dropped the paper on the table.

"Well, let's bring things up to date if that's your aim, Matt. Mrs. O'Donnell's still at it, finds a new friend every time her husband travels to Chicago on business—and guess what? They aren't always man friends."

"Father, don't."

"And how about Peter Mullen? He skims a bit every week at his bank job. Has a system, says he can't stop. No one knows except him and me. And now you.

Satisfied? Is that what your job is now? Gossip? Salacious enough for you, Detective?

"Arthur McDonough has a girlfriend, but she's a transvestite, David Manning keeps a collection of child pornography, and Stella Neary, wait until you hear this one, Matt—"

The swinging door moved. Conley pushed his seat back, stepped quietly, and nudged the heavy door an inch. A dull knock sounded, wood against bone, followed by a groan and the slow shuffle of shoes.

He returned to the table. Father McCarrick was still spouting others' confessions like a sportscaster. His face was flush and perspiration beaded his forehead. Breath came fast.

"Father, stop. Please."

"Why, Matt? I thought you were enjoying it?"

"Tell me about Victor Rodriguez. He went to sex parties?"

McCarrick sat back and rolled his shoulders as if he were trying to scratch an itch against the chair.

"So? He's one of many."

"What did he say about them?"

"Confessors don't elaborate on their sins. 'I did it and here it is, Father. Make it right with a few prayers so I can sin again'."

"What did Victor Rodriguez tell you?" Conley asked.

McCarrick rolled his eyes. "Let's see, he said there was fornication, sodomy, a little S&M, but only on the last week of every month—"

"He actually said those words? Fornication? Sodomy?"

"Matt, I don't take notes on these things. It's too

dark in there to write anyway. I'm giving you the gist."

Mrs. Blodgett pushed through the door with a plate of steaming roast beef, mashed potatoes with gravy, and two crescent rolls. McCarrick moved the newspaper to create an opening in front of him.

The housekeeper turned slightly, looking straight down as if checking her shoes. "Will you be having a plate, Mr. Conley?"

"No, thank you, Mrs. Blodgett. Looks like a nasty bump on your forehead. Might want to be more careful. Kitchen can be a dangerous place."

The housekeeper lifted her chin and left faster than he thought possible.

"I visited Simon O'Neil," Conley said when she'd left.

Father McCarrick held up a fork full of mashed potatoes, gravy dripping. "You are determined to spoil my supper, Matt."

He shrugged. "Sorry. Simon hasn't changed much."

"At least we know it wasn't him painting the statue."

"How do we know that, Father?"

"Because the miracle's real."

Conley peered at him. "You know something."

"No, I don't."

"Yes, you do."

"What will it be now? More blackmail? Headlock maybe? Waterboard?"

"Okay. Tell me one thing. Do you know who did this? Is it related to Victor Rodriguez's murder?"

"That's two things, but I'll give you an opinion anyway, my arithmetic-challenged friend. The miracle is real. The Matt Conley I used to know would have realized that."

He finished the last bite and tore a piece off the roll. He swept the plate with the gravy mop and popped it into his mouth. More pieces, and a dozen swipes later, the plate shone.

Conley stood. He was wasting his time here.

"Going to Morgan's Tap again?" Father McCarrick asked around the last bite.

Conley touched his tender cheek and winced. "Not anytime soon."

Father mumbled, still chewing.

"Too bad."

Chapter 11

On Monday morning, Conley watched crowds funnel up the wide steps of St. Rita's Church for Tommy Lopez's funeral, and squeezed the thick manila envelope in his hand. The mourners angled toward the double front doors, waiting in a queue to step inside. Snowflakes fell on them and clung, as if trying to brighten dark suits and topcoats. The high-pitched chime of a bell sounded three times from inside the church, and its doors closed.

Stefanos and Kendricks watched too, from an unmarked car across the street, breath fogging the windows. Conley snuck toward them, stepped into a doorway hidden from view, and strained to listen to their conversation through Lloyd's partially-open window.

"Big funeral, Captain."

"They're not called funerals anymore. This is a celebration of Tommy's life."

"Shee-it," Kendricks said. "I fucked up. Here I been celebrating his death for three days now."

He started the car. Stefanos threw binoculars into the glove compartment. Conley opened the back door of the cruiser and slid onto the seat.

"Conley?" they erupted in unison.

Conley sat back, legs spread wide, jacket open, the manila envelope against his chest.

"Nippy out there."

"We're on surveillance," Stefanos said. "Get your ass out of here."

"Are you guys aware you're supposed to sit inside the church at a Catholic funeral?"

Kendricks lifted his chin at Conley's cuts and bruises. "Looks like you make friends everywhere you go."

"I'm guessing you don't care who murdered Tommy the Dog. You're here because you think it will help solve Victor Rodriguez's murder."

Kendricks answered. "And I say maybe you ain't as smart of a guesser as you think you are."

"Victor was a wealthy man. Influential. Well-known. Must be a lot of pressure on you guys to show some progress."

"How 'bout you and me step outside and I make some progress kicking your ass?" Kendricks offered.

Stefanos held his hand up.

"But Captain, he's already beat to shit. I can rough this motherfucker up and get away with it 'cause he already looks like hamburger."

Conley waved the envelope in the air. Clasp was open and the yellow strings hung down.

"What's that?" Stefanos asked.

"Victor Rodriguez had a secret. He was into some strange stuff. Dangerous people threatened him."

"Who's your source?"

"Let's just say it's been confirmed by an authority."

Kendricks reached out and tried to swipe the package. Conley pulled it back.

"Whoa," Stefanos said, "Relax, Lloyd. Keep going,

Conley."

"That's it. Not telling you any more, Captain."

"Beating's still on the table, sir," Kendricks said.

"I'm ordering you to give me that information." Stefanos looked irritated.

"Can't order me to do shit, sir. I don't work for you," Conley said.

Kendricks twisted his body, pushed against the steering wheel with his left hand, and braced his whole right arm over the seat back, ready to launch.

"Of course, if I was on the team," Conley said, swinging the envelope from side to side, inches from Kendricks' fingers, "I'd have to share everything I got."

"No way," Kendricks protested. "Don't do it, Captain. He's got nothing we need."

The police scanner squawked. The engine rumbled. Heat hissed from the dashboard vents. Cars drove by, washing the accumulating slush of snow on the street and turning it gray.

Kendricks clenched his fists as he waited for the decision, forehead strained into dark lines, eyes pleading. Clench. Unclench. Clench.

"Okay," Stefanos finally said. "You're in. Be at the station at five o'clock." He pointed at the envelope. "Bring that with you."

Kendricks closed his eyes, rubbed his hand over the short hair on his scalp, and shook his head slowly.

Conley nodded and opened the car door. Cold air and snowflakes blew in and melted on the leather seat. He reached over the seatback and dropped the envelope before he left. "Lloyd can bring it."

Kendricks seized the bottom of the envelope and emptied the contents. Dozens of circulars fell out.

Walmart was having a sale. Two-for-one pizza at Domino's. Sofa Barn was having a going-out-of-business blowout, and this time they were serious.

Conley left the door open and heard Kendricks as he walked away.

"That guy is one grade A fucking asshole."

"But he does have style," Stefanos answered.

****

The snow squall had ended and the sun was shining when Conley parked in front of the condo he and his wife shared—used to share. Hard to think of it as theirs anymore since they'd been living apart. For five weeks now he'd been living a Spartan existence on their cabin cruiser, in the middle of winter no less.

He buzzed in with his keycard and rode the elevator to their place. When Lisa opened the door her eyes went wide.

"Matt, what happened?"

"Reluctant witnesses. Very reluctant."

The dining room table was covered with paper—election speeches, campaign strategy, posters. He saw a memo from Bill McNulty, her campaign manager. Triple exclamation points, quadruple question marks, words in caps, words double-underlined. The guy was even annoying on paper.

He sank into the couch. She went to the kitchen, silk robe swishing.

"Did you go to the hospital?"

"No. A doctor stitched me on her lunch hour."

Lisa came back with a warm facecloth. She washed his face gently, dabbed the blue skin, used her finger to work the cloth around the outside of cuts. He closed his eyes and enjoyed the steamy, healing cloth—or was it the warm hand behind it?

"I can't stay long. We got a lead on the Rodriguez murder."

"That's great, Matt." Her voice hitched. "Honey, I'm so proud of you." Breathing harder now. "So proud."

She drew the facecloth behind his ear and worked it down his neck. She unbuttoned the top of his shirt.

"Where's it hurt?"

"Everywhere."

She smiled. "Really?"

She undressed him as she washed his bruised body. She dropped the facecloth, shrugged her robe off, and lay on him.

Serenity

Was it finally over? Living on the boat, nights falling asleep alone in front of the TV, bizarre counseling sessions with Doctor Larkin?

He hugged her and stared at the vaulted ceiling.

Yellow water stain was still there, souvenir from last fall's Nor'easter. Needed primer and paint.

Lisa lifted her head and her warm breath was on his face.

Refrigerator was awful noisy.

She kissed him, her wet hair clinging to the sides of his face.

A faucet dripped. Somewhere.

Thank God for small problems Father McCarrick had always told him.

Excellent advice.

Chapter 12

Channary looked up from her book. The boys were filing past, feet shuffling, voices silent. Two of them—Vithu and Samay—stopped in the doorway, looking at her and whispering. When Sheila arrived, they hurried away with the rest of their friends. Sheila set an armful of books on the end table and Channary sorted through.

"Sheila, will the policemen ask me more questions about the church?" she asked in Khmer.

"Probably. I'm afraid so. Why?"

"Because there's one question they did not ask."

The basement door at the end of the hall slammed shut. Voices carried from downstairs. Sheila closed the book. "What question?"

"They didn't ask if I prayed. That's what's done in church."

The Aunties passed by on their way to the kitchen. They glanced into the room.

"I'm asking, Channary. Did you pray that night?"

"I did."

The house was silent, except for the murmur from downstairs.

"What did you pray for, Channary?"

Tears formed in Channary's eyes.

"I prayed to be with my family again. I miss Cambodia." She held up a picture book with a cartoon family posing in front of a house. "Like them. Will God

67

answer me, Sheila?"

Thompson took the book from Channary's hands, buried her tears in her shoulder, and took a very long time to answer.

"He will, Channary. I'm sure He will."

****

A grimy basement window was tinged by the setting sun. It cast an eerie orange glow on the shiny black eels that hung from the cellar rafters, waiting to be skinned. Samay thought the light show and the briny smell of the freshly-caught eels formed a strange welcome for this very special Monday night—Pon had finally arrived.

He didn't look like much. Young and thin, with long hair like a girl's. He moved deliberately, like a cat. Face was clean-shaven—perfect skin except for an inch-long crescent-shaped scar across the jut of his chin. The few words he'd uttered so far hadn't been spoken. They'd been purred.

Purred to Samay and Vithu at the bottom of the basement steps as the Asian Boyz passed.

"We robbed Tommy Lopez, the drug dealer," Vithu told Pon breathlessly. "We killed him and destroyed the Latin Kings' club. Ocean Park is ours."

Pon's eyes glittered. "Well done. We'll kill the next drug dealer together."

Vithu froze. Samay caught his breath.

Is Pon a fool? Vithu is Tommy Lopez's replacement. Vithu is the next drug dealer.

Samay filled the growing silence.

"The Latin Kings threatened a Cambodian girl. She's upstairs. Her name is Channary."

Pon's eyebrow rose. "Sounds like something to

fight for."

When the gang had finally gathered, Pon broke away and sat in their middle on an oriental rug so faded from age it was no longer a color. Samay squatted across from him, knees almost to his face, arms wrapped around his calves. The basement was musty even though the nearby furnace labored loudly. Pipes and vents crisscrossed the ceiling, knocking and pinging. Occasionally a swoosh sounded from the thick black soil pipe, or a whoosh from the ancient oil burner.

They were in an open space, but the rest of the basement contained makeshift rooms whose walls were flimsy partitions of two-by-fours and paneling. Thin mattresses lay in the alcoves they formed, along with hotplates, canned food, dishes, and utensils. Burning incense from one of the open rooms mixed with the wetness in the air and smelled like a doused campfire.

Vithu stood guard at the foot of the dark steps, worrying a leather sap. The black weapon seemed to pulse and bulge like it was alive and ready to jump from his hand.

Those in the circle were quiet and still, waiting. The only noise came from overhead—the old women preparing dinner, children playing around them on the kitchen floor. The cellar door creaked open and feet tapped down the stairs. Sleepy had arrived, late as usual, wrinkled clothes hanging on his skinny body. He smiled.

Vithu swung his empty hand in a roundhouse and clapped the newcomer on the side of the face with a sharp slap that hung in the humid air. Vithu then grabbed the boy's collar and flung him toward the open space in the circle beside Samay.

Sleepy dropped to the floor and crossed his legs, the happy smile melting into a frown. A red picture of Vithu's hand covered his cheek. Hair and clothes smelled smoky, like burning leaves. Sleepy was stoned.

Pon nodded, an appraisal and greeting, and scanned the circle one way, then the other. He opened a box, reached inside, and drew out a snake, its wide neck swelled like a vampire's cape. White fangs flashed.

Samay gasped. He'd never seen a snake like this. He'd caught eels in the river—fat, slimy, stupid creatures, but this snake's eyes glowed with intelligence, and seemed to assess them all the same way Pon did.

Vithu prowled outside the circle, the sap squeaking in his hand like a trapped animal. All eyes were on Pon. Looking at Vithu was far too dangerous.

Pon raised a knife in front of the snake's face so that its flickering tongue tapped the metal.

Sleepy giggled. *Maybe no one heard.* The snake's tongue flared.

"A snake questions with its tongue and tastes the air," Pon said. His voice was steady as he turned toward Sleepy's mirth, then nodded.

Suddenly Sleepy was gone. He'd been removed, pulled back fast, as if tethered on a bungee cord.

Samay chanced a look behind. Vithu was dragging Sleepy along the cement floor, arms and legs flailing. They disappeared into a cubicle.

Pon tapped the top of the snake's head. Its mouth opened and hissed wetly—the promise of venom.

"Well armed, but harmless if contained," he said, tapping again, with the same response.

A sharp thwack sounded in the cubicle, and a

muffled cry—or had the sound come from above?

Fear brought on denial. *Maybe footsteps of the old women working in the kitchen, maybe a finger burned on a hot stove?*

Pon raised the snake and stroked its underbelly with the dull edge of the knife. The snake's tongue slowed.

"He wants safety and pleasure. Comfort."

More sounds from the cubicle, thuds and bangs. A groan followed.

Maybe not from behind. Maybe the children upstairs, wrestling on the kitchen floor, scuffling.

Pon turned the knife suddenly, so quickly the blade seemed part of his hand. He cut the snake's head off with a blinding flick and threw the writhing, bleeding body into the box. The head tumbled onto the rug and landed in the middle of the circle. Its mouth opened and closed. The boys stared.

Vithu returned and sat next to Samay, his chest heaving. The veins in his muscular neck and on the backs of his bony, tattooed hands were dark and full, as if they lay on his skin instead of under it.

"Snakes are brave warriors," Pon said. "Even after they die, they fight. Their poison lives."

The others stared, transfixed. Vithu's heavy breath warmed Samay's neck. Sleepy whimpered in the cubicle. But when Pon cast his unblinking cat eyes on Samay it felt as if they were the only ones in the room.

"We must prepare," Pon said to him, his voice as smooth as the downy cheeks it came from. "Snakes are coming."

Chapter 13

March felt like February. The frosted windows in the squad room radiated an icy draft. On Tuesday morning Conley flipped to a new page in his notebook and waited for the daily brief to begin.

"Arson," Mazzarelli said, pushing his glasses with an index finger and stretching his arms. "According to the Fire Marshal, there's no doubt. The Hispanic Social Club was destroyed intentionally. Utility company showed a 10-minute spike in demand for no good reason, which means the gas line was cut. Neighbors heard a gunshot that probably ignited the gas. Must have been an incendiary round."

"What's the link to this investigation?" Stefanos asked.

"Unclear, maybe nothing. Maybe coincidence. Victor Rodriguez was a founder of the club, helped fund its construction. By the way, the building was underinsured. Never had an inflation rider. Rebuilding would cost twice the payout."

"Wasn't he an insurance man?" one of the other detectives asked.

"Barber always needs a haircut," Stefanos answered. "What else do we have?"

"Substance on the statue was blood—bovine."

"Cow?"

"Yes, sir."

Kendricks leaned toward him. "We need to be questioning cows, Captain?"

The other cops snickered.

"Keep going, Mazzarelli."

"Detective Conley has been cleared of wrongdoing at the Rodriguez murder scene. Police union got involved and negotiated a confession from Detective Jackson in exchange for an early retirement package."

"So we paid a policeman to tell the truth," Stefanos said. "That's wonderful."

Mazzarelli handed a sheaf of stapled pages to Conley. "You need to sign these. Confirmation of the story you told, releases to Detective Jackson from recourse."

Conley nodded, fished in his jacket for a pen, and read the top page of the report. Blocks of legal text cascaded under the Ocean Park Police logo, and Jackson's name appeared about a hundred times in bold caps.

"Open items, Mazzarelli?"

"I'm researching Conley's story about the Paladin sex club. Nothing yet. No hits in our database."

"Sex club?" Kendricks asked, giving Conley the stink eye. "Sounds like bullshit."

"Primary meaning of the word paladin is a heroic champion," Mazzarelli said. "We think this one is the secondary meaning—stately mansion."

"What else?"

"Lots of leads, Captain. I made a list."

Stefanos laid his pen down.

"Kendricks. You pair up with Conley and see Channary and the social worker. Bring Conley up to speed on the investigation while you're at it."

Mazzarelli's pen was poised like a dart.

Kendricks looked up from his notepad.

"Not a good idea, sir."

"I didn't ask if it was."

But Kendricks was undaunted. "Better I go see the girl alone, one on one, y'know, less intimidating."

Stefanos' voice took on a steely edge. "I gave you an order, Detective." He cast a long stare at Kendricks, who ran his open hand down his face.

"Yes, sir."

Mazzarelli lowered his Bic and recorded the assignment.

****

Kendricks walked fast through the parking lot. Conley was right behind. He pointed at his BMW, black paint gleaming.

"We can take my car."

"Not an option."

They reached Kendricks' sedan and he unlocked the doors with his key fob, pressing the button hard, before he yanked open the driver's door and hauled himself inside.

"I guess you're driving, then," Conley said amicably, opening the passenger door and leaning in as Kendricks fastened his seat belt.

"And if your ass ain't buckled into that seat in three seconds, you won't be ridin'."

"I'm all for personal safety. Mind if we make a stop?"

"No. I'm pointing the fuckin' car, I'm deciding where to go, and you're along to waste gas and breathin' air."

"I'm just trying to get along here, Kendricks."

"Detective Kendricks is the name, and you can try whatever you want, motherfucker. But I ain't stopping this bus until we get where the captain said to go."

Conley grabbed the steering wheel at the three o'clock position and held tight.

"One stop on the way."

Seconds ticked by. A pedestrian passed in front of them, the click of his shoes like a metronome. The sun's fading light shone through the grimy windshield.

Kendricks' voice was low with fury, each word pronounced separately. "Take your hand off my wheel."

"Listen to me, Kendricks. This is my home, my town. A man was killed in my church, and the city I've loved and lived in my whole life is disintegrating right in front of me. Know this: I'm going to find Victor Rodriguez's killer—and the Hispanic Club's arsonist—with or without your help."

Kendricks gave a long stare. Conley took his hand off the wheel.

"One stop." Kendricks started the car.

"That's right."

"Just the one."

Kendricks spun the wheel and aimed toward the parking lot exit. "Better not be no Starbucks, Mr. BMW. Ain't never been there and don't plan on startin' up."

"Nope."

They reached the exit. "Then mind telling me which way we're going?"

"Straight to hell. Morgan's Tap."

"Morgan's Tap?" Kendricks closed his eyes and flexed his hands. "Shee-it."

****

Morgan's was crowded. The fat tires of a long line of gleaming Harleys kissed the curb. The Tap's tattered front door was working hard, swallowing bikers and barflies.

Kendricks parked across the street and reached for the police microphone.

"What are you doing?" Conley asked.

"Calling for backup. Even then I ain't sure this is a good idea."

Conley placed his hand over the mic. "We don't need it here. Trust me." He hopped out of the car and headed past the fleet of gleaming chrome and rubber. Kendricks hustled to catch up.

They opened the door and walked into smoke and noise. The sweet smell of marijuana mixed with the too-loud sound of heavy metal rock. All was well in the Tap. Donna sat at her video game, cigarette between her lips, beer mug balanced on her lap. Rocco was on his stool, wide awake, hands working as he spoke at patrons on both sides. Teddy was busy serving, his face sweating.

Kendricks caught Conley by the arm. "We're out of here. Now. I already counted three of the most wanted guys in the state, one of them suspected in a triple homicide."

"Don't worry. It's safe."

"Christ. You got some kind of fucked up suicide wish?" He reached into his jacket and kept his hand on his holster. "Death by biker mob wasn't on my dance card today."

There it is again. Prove yourself. Show me. Convince me you're not the fuck-up everyone says you are.

"So be it."

Conley walked over to big Tony just as Teddy was delivering a beer, and elbowed the biker so hard he almost fell off the stool.

"Yep," Kendricks muttered under his breath, "that's the triple homicide."

Conley reached in front of Tony and slid three fingers into the mug handle. He lifted the beer, drank, and slammed the half-empty glass down so hard the rest of the brew splashed onto the front of the biker's T-shirt.

Tony never moved.

"What the—?"

"Told you, Kendricks. It's safe."

With that, Conley headed toward William O'Neil's office. Halfway there, he looked back over his shoulder. Kendricks was following—tentatively—hand on his service pistol, one eye on the patrons at the bar, one eye on his crazy new partner.

Chapter 14

On Wednesday Father McCarrick climbed the steps to the landing in front of the church. He smoothed his cassock, not that it had wrinkles. Mrs. Blodgett didn't allow them. His housekeeper pressed clothes as well as she cooked. She worked an iron strong and fast, steam puffing from the machine that breathed as hard as she did.

A car pulled in front of the Church of St. Ambrose, a little foreign job with a donut replacement for a front wheel and a plastic flower atop the antenna. A girl got out, supersized pocketbook slung over one arm, camera dangling from a lanyard around her neck. She dropped keys into the big bag, and fished out pad and pen as she climbed the concrete steps. She offered a limp hand and they shook.

"Sorry I'm late, Father. Debbie Feldman."

One side of his mouth curled. "Not a problem, my dear. God loves the tardy too."

He held the door open and she stepped into the vestibule. He touched the holy water in the bowl that hung from the wall, blessing himself as she watched.

"I take it you're not Catholic, dear?"

"Jewish."

"Beautiful religion. We have something in common—the Old Testament."

She scratched her head and smoothed disheveled

black hair before scribbling a note and pointing to the statue of St. Ambrose.

"Is that the Madonna?"

A smile. "No, dear, that's our St. Ambrose, a pious and eloquent man. One of the first Doctors of Catholic theology."

She looked around, pulled the door open to the church proper, and stepped inside.

He moved quickly and caught the door before it closed. "Go right in, my dear. Step right in."

She was already at the last row of benches, looking toward the faraway altar, then up at the painted ceiling. She turned and looked at the choir, the balcony wall with its carved curves, crenellations, and curlicues, and the bank of gold pipes, a giant pan flute turned on end.

"Very ornate," she said.

"All to glorify God, my dear. Glory to the Father."

"Where'd Victor Rodriguez die?"

He folded his hands and closed his eyes. "A beautiful man, Victor. Such a pity. Frightening thing, really."

"I heard it was up front. Near the altar."

She set off down the wide main aisle, shoes slapping tile. He hustled to keep up, short legs making the bottom of his cassock dance. He pointed to the windows as he jogged.

"The stained glass, Ms. Feldman. Imported from Germany a hundred years ago. Back before the Germans got caught up in that World War business." Hesitation. "No need to remind you about that, I imagine."

She stole a glance at the overhead lights and adjusted the wheel on her camera.

"Invaluable art, Stations of the Cross we call them. Same as the windows in the cathedral at Cologne."

She slung her behemoth of a pocketbook into a pew and it clunked heavily on the wood.

"First row, right?" she asked. "Which seat?"

He pointed at the seat near the aisle, the last seat Victor Rodriguez ever occupied. She raised the camera and the flash fired, bleaching the wood.

"We usually don't allow cameras, Ms. Feldman, except for weddings. But I guess this is all right."

She stood at different angles, shooting the seat in portrait and landscape orientations, near and far.

"Altar's Italian marble, from the Carrara quarry in Tuscany. Same as St. Peter's, you know. I've always wanted to go there. St. Peter's I mean, not Tuscany, though I suppose I should visit both."

She moved next to him, still hunting for the perfect angle to shoot Victor Rodriguez's dying spot. He caught a whiff of stale coffee and stepped out of her way.

"The church is closing, you know. Heartbreaking for the parishioners, what's left of them anyway. Cardinal's trying to convince us to combine with St. Margaret's over on the west side. Never happen."

She turned to the altar, aimed quickly, and snapped a single picture.

"I heard."

"We're hoping the Archdiocese reconsiders, what with the history and beauty you've just seen. I hope you include that in your story. Subtly, of course. No quotes or anything."

"Which one's the Madonna?"

He bowed his head, raised an arm weakly, and

started toward the side altar. She passed him and stopped. He caught up.

"Would you like to light a candle, Ms. Feldman?"

She stared down at the bank of votive glasses, most of them empty, glass blackened, burnt wicks lying on the bottom. Two contained lit candles, one flickering, threatened by the liquid pool of wax it created. She drew a long taper from a holder, caught flame from the weak candle, and lit a fresh one.

He searched his pocket for change and found none. He placed his empty closed fist on the coin slot of the offertory can and shook the whole thing. The change inside rattled.

"Father, tell me about the miracle."

"Pardon?"

She looked up at the statue. "When Victor Rodriguez's body was found, the statue was crying."

"Who told you that, Ms. Feldman?"

"I heard the tears were red, like blood." She leaned over the candles to inspect the Madonna, stepped back, and refocused her camera. "I need a picture."

"Of course." He stepped in front of the candles and smoothed his robe. One hand on the rail, he lifted his chin the way Mrs. Blodgett had told him to, so neck and jowls were taut.

She lowered the camera. "I meant of the statue."

He grunted and walked a half circle until he was standing behind her.

"Do you deny the miracle, Father?"

"I like to think miracles happen every day, Ms. Feldman."

"Not like this one, I think. What action is the Archdiocese taking?"

"You'll have to ask them, my dear."

She nodded. "I plan to."

She retrieved her heavy bag and slung it over the shoulder so it was bouncing on her back as she walked the main aisle. She fished keys and a pack of cigarettes out of it, and clutched them as she elbowed the door to the vestibule. He was close behind, breathing hard.

"Sorry my answers weren't specific, Ms. Feldman," he said as they burst through the front door into the sunlight.

"Don't worry about it."

"I'm just very discreet, that's all. Nothing personal. My training, you see. Vows and all that."

She lit a cigarette and turned to face the church.

"Exactly how long have you been here, Father—at St. Ambrose?"

"Couple of decades."

She nodded, braced her bag, and skipped down the stairs to her car.

"Seat of the Archdiocese is in Southie now, my dear," he called. "Be careful. Traffic around South Station is hellacious."

She slammed her car door and started the ignition. White smoke plumed from the tailpipe. A rev made the pipe shimmy and the muffler blatted like a sour trumpet note. She shifted into gear and drove away.

"Nice girl," he said to himself in spite of her impoliteness. She hadn't thanked him for his time and never even bid a proper farewell. No matter. Everyone needed forgiveness for something.

"God bless," he said to the loud little car that created clouds behind it. "God bless, Ms. Feldman."

Chapter 15

Conley sat next to William O'Neil's desk. Outside the office, Morgan's Tap was alive with customers on a busy Thursday, exhaling smoke tinged with the sweet smell of alcohol.

Drawings lined the walls, large sketches taped to the wood paneling. Conley and Kendricks studied the gallery. Sage and O'Neil studied the detectives.

William pointed at a drawing of a building, a stark, windowless gray box with steps attached. He touched its middle with bent knuckles.

"That's it, Matt. The Paladin."

Sage stood, placed her hand on O'Neil's shoulder, and drew it lovingly across as she passed.

That touch is more than just friendship, Conley thought.

She tapped the top of the portraits. "And these are its members."

The faces shared the same pose, as if they were staring straight into a photographer's lens. Names were drawn under each one, beautiful curling titles done in calligraphy. They made the subjects look regal.

"I drew them from memory," she said. "Thought they might help."

She continued around the room, palms smoothing some, fingers flicking others, a checkmark of approval.

"Some of these people will help us find out who

threatened Victor. Carrie's one who'll talk for sure. Others won't. Some will want to stop us from learning anything."

"The pictures will definitely help," Conley said. "So where is the Paladin?"

Sage and O'Neil exchanged glances, as if deciding who would answer.

"We have no idea," O'Neil said.

"I don't understand."

"Victor drove," she said. "I went only twice, never paid attention to its location."

"Just ask one of them," Conley said. He swung his arm at the portraits.

"Victor knew them. I don't know how to contact any of these people," Sage said.

"I can find their club," O'Neil said.

"No, William," Conley said. "That's my job."

Sage sat, crossed her legs, folded her arms, and eyed Conley.

"May I make a suggestion?" O'Neil asked.

"No need," Conley said. "You've been a great help already. Thank you both."

Amateur hour's over.

He stood and motioned Kendricks to leave.

"Matt—"

"Forget it, William. We'll let you know what happens," Conley said as he and Kendricks shrugged into their jackets and turned to leave.

Sage shook her head and folded her arms.

Chapter 16

That same afternoon, the bell rang outside Conley's cabin cruiser, and he unzipped the tarp. Sage stood on the dock.

"Sage. Didn't expect to see you." He offered a hand to help her aboard. "Come in."

She stepped onto the deck tentatively, carrying a large sketchpad under her arm, and followed him into the cabin. He checked the thermostat and turned up the propane heater.

"You live on a boat in Seaport Marina in the winter?" she said. "Interesting."

"Not by choice. My wife and I are separated, but not by much. She got the better end, the condo at the other end of the marina."

"I made more sketches of the people at the parties. Despite your unwillingness to let him help, William thought I should show them to you."

Conley let that sleeping dog lie. There was a history there he didn't care to go into. "What have you got?"

She sat on the bench across from him and opened the pad. The pages were so big they created a breeze when turned. She stopped at a full-faced woman with a tangle of wavy hair, broad nose, and thin lips.

Sage pinched a charcoal pencil between thumb and fingertips, and ran it under the picture's chin in a U, barely touching the page. Satisfied, she lifted her hand and spoke.

"Carrie's her name. She knew Victor."

"She looks sad."

Sage smiled. "Then I've succeeded. That's the hard part, you know. Making the picture come alive."

The bubbler hummed under the hull, its prop turning constantly to prevent the bilge from freezing. The propane heater hissed. She turned the page.

A thin-faced man with a devil's goatee was next. His hair receded on both sides of his forehead, as if making way for horns.

"That's Liam. Everyone's scared of him, and they should be. He gets what he wants, doesn't tolerate bullshit. Gets rough with the girls sometimes. The willing and the unwilling."

"Is he the one who threatened Victor Rodriguez?"

"I think so."

She ran the charcoal around Liam's oval eyes, then looked at Conley's as if comparing. "Sit down. I need to take your stitches out or they'll leave scars."

He sat on the bed. She turned her chair, searched her bag, pulled out scissors and tweezers. She touched his eyebrows, worried the ends of the black stitches, cut them carefully, and pulled them through.

"How long have you and William known each other?" she asked.

"Forever."

A long pull on the middle stitch. He winced.

"We were pretty close at one time," he said.

She concentrated on a cut near his eye and rubbed her thumb against a spot as if trying to erase it.

"When we're young, our heart is like clay. It gets

molded from experiences, good and bad. Did you and William have a good relationship?"

"Yes."

"He seeks your approval."

He shrugged. "I like William."

"Then why do you treat him like shit?"

He smiled, eyes shut, lips closed.

"He's a good man," she said. "God-fearing, and wise beyond his years. He saved me, rescued me from an empty life."

"William needs to know there are boundaries, that's all. He can't show up in Ocean Park after a decade and think he's going to be a hero."

"Right. I see. Because that's you. You're the one who's going to fix things, and he's getting in your way."

"That's not true."

She broke a capsule and rubbed fluid on the cuts.

"You know what my mother used to say, Conley? Love is not about sex or beauty or tenderness. It's about being one. Momma said she and my daddy were so in love they could speak without words to each other and see without sight. William and I used to do that."

"What happened?"

"You showed up. Now all William cares about is helping you. It's like he owes you a debt, and it's affecting him and me. We're distant now."

A debt? That wasn't it. Truth was the young William was a runt, often bullied, always teased. Was he ever cowardly? Not that Conley could remember, but that didn't matter because the seed of mistrust, a lack of confidence, was planted way back—*when we were clay*—and no amount of war stories could blunt that feeling.

Or is Sage right? Is he getting in my selfish way?

"I'm sorry," he said. "But I can't deal with William right now. I know he wants to help. I'll keep that in mind."

She tilted her head.

"That's one of God's little jokes on us, you know. We're links in a long, hanging chain. We cling to the loop above us, desperate to be one with them, but the link below hangs on us the same way, and we don't even notice."

She smoothed his eyebrow over the red skin.

"Sometimes letting friends help is the hardest thing we do," she said. "It takes all of our courage."

A voice called from the dock.

"Everything all right in there, Mister Conley?" Buddy, the busybody marina manager, asked clear and slow.

"Yeah, Buddy. Everything's okay."

"You're sure?"

"Yes, Buddy. Sage was just leaving."

Sage stood, tucked the portfolio under her arm, and buttoned her coat. "If you really want to save this city," she said, "and from what I can see, it needs a lot of help—you'll need William."

Conley reached, held her hand still, and spoke.

"I can't promise that, Sage."

She sighed.

"That's God's other joke, you know. He puts fantasies in our head, windmills. Then He makes us want them so bad we'll do anything. When we succeed, we wonder why we ever wanted the silly thing, and God laughs so hard even we can hear. Momma used to say that's called thunder."

She stepped out onto the deck, and with his help climbed the transom to the dock. She turned.

"Better keep an eye on those cuts, Conley. Your blood seems thin. You'll probably bleed again."

Chapter 17

Kendricks shouted Conley's name from the dock the next morning. Conley lifted the boat cover and peered out. The day was coming hard, the top part of the sun already sitting on the Atlantic horizon like a half-eaten peach. Ice caked the pier and packed the spaces between the deck boards. Spring was only weeks away—hard to believe when Ocean Park was still frozen as the Arctic.

Kendricks whistled. "Your boat?"

Conley grabbed his coat and they headed for Lisa's condo. "Like it? My wife and I bought it on our anniversary."

"Not bad. I got a boat too."

"Stinkpot?"

Kendricks stepped back. "It ain't no fucking albino martini boat like this ark, and I don't wear alligator golf shirts when I drive it."

"Don't take it personal. Stinkpot means power boat. Sailboats are called rag merchants."

"Oh. Yeah. Well, I got a power boat. My wife and kids say it smells awful bad, so maybe it is a stinkpot after all."

The steel beams and angled glass of the condo building gleamed in the new sun, which had climbed and cleared the water line by the time they reached the lobby. The walls were decorated with nautical artifacts—brass diving helmet, paintings of sea battles, conch shells in glass cases. They crossed the lobby and stepped into the empty elevator. Floor numbers flashed overhead.

"Martini boat," Conley said, smiling.

"Seemed to fit the situation."

The elevator stopped and they stepped into the hallway. Flowers decorated accent tables and fake portholes hung on every door.

Conley fit his key into the lock of his condo, twisted the key, and turned the knob.

Lisa sat at the breakfast table in the silk robe he'd bought her for Christmas, the one she'd been wearing the last time he'd seen her—the last time they'd made love. The French doors behind her framed the harbor.

"Matt, what are you doing here?" She set her coffee cup in its saucer.

"Any coffee left, honey? This is Lloyd Kendricks. We're working the Rodriguez murder."

A drawer closed in the bathroom. The toilet flushed.

Conley paused. "Who's here?"

Before she could answer, Bill McNulty strolled into the living room. He wore Conley's bathrobe, the white one with the red anchor over the heart.

"Lisa?"

Why?

Didn't they have a great life together? *Why* flush all that down a noisy toilet? *Why* turn your back on someone who loves you so very, very much? The dull ache he felt when he thought about losing her grew into white-hot pain.

Why?

"You'd better go," McNulty said. He set his skinny shoulders back and spread his hands on the granite kitchen counter.

Kendricks stepped closer. "Talking might be a bad idea right now, Romeo."

McNulty frowned. "Don't leave without giving me name and badge number, Officer. I golf with the District Attorney. He likes to know which of his guys have smart mouths." He poured coffee into Conley's BOSTON cup.

"Matt, please leave," Lisa said. "We'll talk later."

Her words created a deafening roar in his head. She was all he'd ever wanted—that and to have kids with her same cocoa eyes. Raise them in Ocean Park, watch them play baseball at Frey Field, maybe cheer in the old stadium. Watch them play and grow and laugh. Watch them run on long tanned legs—like Lisa's.

He lifted his head and turned to McNulty. "I want my bathrobe."

McNulty took a sip of coffee. One eyebrow rose and fell. "Sure. Nice material, by the way."

He took a step toward the bedroom. Conley blocked his way.

"Now."

"Matt," Lisa said, loud and clear, like a mother scolding her child.

"Don't make this worse for everybody, Conley."

"I just want the robe. Then I'll leave."

McNulty stepped away from him, as if moving toward Lisa, but instead angled toward the front door. Kendricks caught his intent and leaned against the doorjamb, arms crossed.

"Massachusetts State Police Detective Lloyd

Kendricks, badge number 63925."

McNulty paused, then drifted back to the center of the room and looked to Lisa. He scratched the back of his neck.

"Lisa?"

She looked away.

Conley stepped to him, snagged his comfortable robe by the fluffy collar—*nice material*—and shucked it down, peeled it right off. McNulty's arms shot straight back and came together briefly at the wrists as if he were being cuffed.

McNulty stood naked. His body was pale, pubic hair trimmed and flecked with gray. Man boobs and a paunch hung from his skinny frame.

"Really, Lisa?"

Conley held the robe at arm's length—as if it still contained a vile politician—walked toward the balcony past his cheating, coffee-drinking wife, and opened the French doors. Brisk air poured in, but it had a hint of warmth, a harbinger of spring.

He flung the robe toward the harbor, and it flattened in the air and cartwheeled slowly. The sleeves fluttered as if searching for balance. The bathrobe landed in the water and spread out, heart print down, in a dead man's float.

McNulty crossed his hands in front of his crotch. Conley approached and spoke.

"Get your own damn bathrobe."

He turned toward the front door. Kendricks stepped aside and opened the door wide. Conley strode through it, disappointed there wasn't a nosey neighbor passing by in that moment, to witness McNulty in all his naked glory.

"I guess we're done here?" Kendricks asked quietly once they'd reached the elevator.

"Yes, Lloyd. We're done."

Conley punched the button to the elevator. A second later he punched it again, harder. They got in and the quiet elevator passed floors slowly, blinking white buttons counting down.

"'Get your own damn bathrobe'," Kendricks said. "I liked that."

Eye number one brightened as the door opened to the well-appointed lobby.

Conley smiled. "So did I."

Chapter 18

Conley and Kendricks left the condo and drove along the beach road, past high, undulating stands of sea oats. The sand was wet and dark, with patches of smoky snow that matched the gray crests of winter waves.

Conley knew his marriage was over. Problem was his heart thought otherwise and kept rationalizing, explaining, holding hope. Hearts weren't very smart. Every part of him ached and the roar in his head had turned into a debilitating migraine.

Kendricks headed downtown and ran leads on Victor Rodriguez's murder. Conley waited silently in the car and listened as Kendricks filled him in on interviews with Rodriguez's barber, dentist, brother-in-law. Victor was well-coiffed for his murder, had nary a cavity in that whitened smile, and by the way, when's the reading of the will?

Late in the morning Kendricks turned the sedan toward Ocean Park Highlands. Its big engine chewed the hill easily, and made the car bank around corners like an Olympic sprinter. They passed houses Conley had known since childhood, but today they seemed different, as if holding secrets. Were his eyes liars or were those colonials watching him? A-frame roofs formed furrowed brows, matching pairs of windows stared like eyes, front porches smirked as if the slanted boards were a mocking row of teeth. Catching your wife with her lover had a lot of weird effects—like making sticks and bricks look suspicious.

They climbed a steep hill, entered an older section of well-kept colonials and bungalows, and parked in front of a small green house, plain and neat. Two kids tottered through snow banks in the front yard, tiny Michelin men in fat down jackets. They heaved snowballs at icicles hanging from house gutters, leaning back so far to throw they looked like shot putters.

"Where are we?" Conley asked.

"My house."

"Why?"

"Lunch time, that's why."

Kendricks called to the kids and they waddled over to meet their dad's new partner.

Leshawn was tall and skinny, the bill of a baseball cap sticking out from his tight hood, shading shy eyes that looked mostly down. Kit, the younger one, stared at Conley as if trying to hypnotize him.

A tall, attractive woman in paint-splattered jeans and sweatshirt stood at the front door.

"My wife Madie," Kendricks said as he kissed her cheek. "Works like the devil around the house, but not like you'd think. She's all hammers and paint brushes, that girl."

"And Lloyd's all laundry baskets and baking recipes. We call it role reversal."

Lloyd held the door open and rolled his eyes.

"Now don't go tellin' my secrets, woman."

They walked through a tidy hallway, past a formal living room, and into a kitchen with a big table. A bay window overlooked a small yard and a deck with a grill covered in a black tarp, a round cap of snow on top. The yard was desolate. Bare, snow-frosted trees were the only sign life had ever existed there.

Kendricks retrieved an armful of food from the refrigerator, headed for the back porch, and uncovered the grill. Madie set flowered placemats and napkins on the table as the boys climbed into seats. Conley pointed at Leshawn's blank baseball cap.

"We need to get you a Red Sox hat."

"Leshawn don't want no letters or nothing on his hat," Kit said. "Makes people want to talk to him—askin' about the team and all. He hates that."

Leshawn frowned at his brother.

"Kit, quiet down," Madie said. "Leshawn can speak for himself to Mister Conley."

"Blank hat's not a bad idea," Conley said. "Keeps everyone guessing who you like."

"Leshawn don't like talking to no one," Kit said. "Teacher says he's ant-social."

"Shut up," Leshawn said in a strained whisper, stretching the "up" to a multi-syllable word with many octaves.

"I'm the same way," Conley said. "Too many people talk when they got nothing to say. Wastes all the oxygen."

"You ant-social too?"

Madie leaned forward. "Kit Kendricks, why don't you and your brother do something useful and help your daddy?"

The kids slid off their seats and Leshawn gave his little brother a knuckle on the back of the head that sounded as loud as a hammer on wood.

"Leshawn's still adjusting," she said when they

left. "He's quiet. We moved here last summer. He hasn't made a lot of friends."

"Where'd you live?"

"Jacksonville. South as the South gets."

"Why'd you move?"

"Captain Stefanos met Lloyd on a case and offered him a job. Best thing ever happened to that man. I can't say much for the cold and snow, but Lloyd's a lot happier and we feel safe here."

"Jacksonville that bad?"

"North part is, where we lived. Murder capital of Florida most years. Dangerous place. And when you go to the west side, rebel flags on pickup trucks let you know where those boys stand."

Kendricks and his sons came in with a plate of hamburgers. They sat around the table, waiting for everyone to be served.

"Ketchup, please," Kit said.

Conley passed the squeeze bottle.

"That's mighty white of you," Kit said.

Madie dropped her hamburger. "Kittredge Quentin Kendricks. Apologize right now."

"For what? He is white."

"You're not supposed to say that," Leshawn whispered. Kit frowned as he bit into his hamburger.

The Kendricks family ate in silence and traded threatening stares.

"Tastes like summer," Conley said suddenly.

"How can a hamburger taste like summer?" Kit asked.

Conley pointed out the window at bony, bare branches on a maple tree.

"Tastes like a warm breeze on a hot day when the

wind blows through those big fat leaves hanging off that tree."

Kit put an elbow on the table, turned, and peered outside.

"Rolls taste warm too, like they've been sitting in that July sun outside. And the tomatoes are juicy and sweet. Probably just got picked out of the garden back there. They kinda smell like that honeysuckle blooming on the fence."

Kit turned to his mother and cupped a hand to his mouth. He used the index finger on his other hand to make circles next to his head. "He's nuts."

"Kit, apologize."

"I'm sorry he's nuts."

"I'm just trying to fool Mother Nature, that's all," Conley said. "Maybe I can get her to bring summer faster so you can go out on your daddy's new boat."

Kendricks raised an eyebrow.

Kit's eyes widened. "Hey, if we went out on the boat, maybe Granny Nature would think summer was here and make the principal end school early for the year."

"Mother Nature," Leshawn said. "Not Granny."

"Granny's a mother too."

"I'm sure stranger things have happened," Conley said.

"All right. We're going out on Dad's boat." Kit pointed a ketchup-covered finger at Conley. "He said so."

"Too cold to go on the boat," Madie said. She squinted at her husband. "Besides, we don't even know if it runs."

"It runs," Kendricks says. "Engine starts and the

propeller turns, woman. That's all she needs to do."

"Sounds like you need a shakedown cruise," Conley said.

"What's that?" Kit asked.

"Trial run. Make sure everything works well. Steering, bilge pump, lights."

"In the winter?"

"Sure. Better, actually. No other boats around to get in the way."

"Can we do a shakedown?" Kit asked his mother.

Madie shook her head. "Seems awful cold to be out on a boat"—she eyed her husband—"a very suspect boat."

"We'll just be on the river," Conley said. "Hard to get in much trouble there."

"Might be fun," Lloyd told her.

Madie turned her neck as if working a crick. "That kind of fun sounds like the worst kind—cheap, easy, and dangerous."

Kendricks frowned.

Kit stared at her wide-eyed as he stuffed the last piece of hamburger into his mouth. Leshawn waited for her answer too. He adjusted his cap with both hands, trying to curve the bill.

She smiled at her husband.

"Well, all right. I always was a sucker for cheap and easy."

Chapter 19

Two days later, Conley and Kendricks visited the River Street tenement, and followed an old Cambodian woman whose long, rust-colored dress whispered. A gold sash circled her ample waist, a silk crown on hips that swayed like a ship on rolling seas. The hallway walls were the color of candy apples, the trim a bright orange, floors painted lemon yellow.

They passed a room with benches and smoky incense burners that fogged a statue of Buddha. Kitchen sounds grew loud as they neared the end of the corridor—a splash in a sink, the hiss of boiling water, chop of a knife on a cutting board. They turned into the big kitchen and were greeted by the backs of a half-dozen working women.

Channary and Sheila Thompson sat on stools at a butcher block island, mixing paste in a bowl with wooden spoons. The young girl's eyes were as bright as Conley remembered. They brightened more when she saw him.

Thompson slid off her stool and greeted them.

"Welcome to Cambodia West, Detectives. Channary's learning English fast. She had some lessons at the orphanage. I'm teaching her to read."

A woman eyed them and quickly turned back to cleaning dishes.

"Can we talk with her?" Conley asked.

"No talk," the woman at the sink barked. Her round, sweaty face flashed over her shoulder. "Work."

Channary was shucking corn now, throwing husks in a bag on the floor.

"Do either of you speak French?" Thompson whispered.

"I know a bit," Kendricks said. "Cajun variety."

"They say Channary's too busy to talk. The only way I'll get them to leave is for a holy man. Do your Sunday best, Detective Kendricks. Their English is sketchy, but they know French."

"There's one problem. They ain't Baptist."

"They're not fussy when it comes to salvation." Sheila turned to the women, waved her arms, and called "*un saint homme*" in singsong. She pointed to Kendricks.

"*Ecoutez.* Holy man, ladies. *Ecoutez.*"

Kendricks stepped forward.

"*Bienvenue a la Dieu, mes soeurs. Bienvenue.*" He placed his big hand on his chest and it almost reached shoulder to shoulder. His free hand shot toward the ceiling like a preacher's. "Alleluia!"

One by one the women waddled out of the kitchen, past the giant black man who beckoned them with a strange, impassioned drawl. Thompson herded them to the hallway and shouted "*Shaman!*" to the laggards.

Kendricks followed the shuffling women up to the prayer room, voice dropping an octave every time he spoke Cajun, arms open as if to encircle his new flock.

Sheila stepped back to the counter and put her hand over the girl's. "You've got your time, Detective Conley. Channary's English is coming along, but she talks in idioms—riddles if you will. They can be hard to decipher."

"I'll manage," he said.

Channary was chopping now, peppers as big as grapefruit. She held a large knife, both hands on the worn handle.

He pulled a stool in front of her and sat. She pressed down on a big bell pepper and it scurried away from the knife and rolled across the cutting table. Conley caught it before it fell.

"Channary, what did you see when you walked into the church that night—the night we met?"

She looked past his shoulder and selected an onion from a basket. She hacked it open and the stinging scent filled the air between them.

"Aunties were flying," she said.

Conley hesitated and turned to Thompson.

"Those are the Aunties," she told Conley, jerking her thumb toward the women who'd left. "That's what she calls them. Channary says they look like the saints on the church ceiling. They have flowing robes."

"And a man," she said suddenly. "He came down from the altar."

"What did he look like?" Conley said.

"I sat in a tall deadbox, so I could barely see."

"Deadbox?" he said.

"She hid in the confessional," Thompson said, "a box like an upright coffin." She smiled. "That one was kind of easy."

A dozen questions—a dozen puzzling answers.

Kendricks' shouts rang from the prayer room, his voice booming now, switching between English and French. He sounded like he was singing backup for himself.

"Welcome the Lord into your life every day, ladies, so He'll welcome you on your last. *Vous venez a Dieu.*"

The incense smoke was seeping into the kitchen. Channary rubbed her eyes and coughed. She slid off the stool and stretched to get a glass from the cabinet.

"*La Dieu est venire.*"

Lloyd sang *Amazing Grace* in a deep, rich voice that seemed to carry on the sweet-smelling smoke. Conley ran his hand down his face. If progress were to be measured by the number of meaningless, disconnected facts collected, he was doing well.

Conley closed his eyes.

We're going to need more than prayer, Kendricks, because we're getting nowhere. Playing games.

"Your partner has talent, Conley. These ladies have low tolerance for the uninspiring. He's doing well."

Kendricks returned and the ladies went back to work.

"We need to go," Conley told him. "We're wasting time."

"Wait," Thompson said. "I found out more about Channary. Friends International traced her to a nasty orphanage in Kompong Cham. They also tracked her family."

"Family? You said she was in an orphanage."

"Most kids in Cambodian orphanages have parents who are just too poor to keep them. Unfortunately, many of these places are preyed on by the orphan tourists. Predators pay a few dollars to get in and check out the kids. Somebody took a liking to Channary and 'adopted' her."

"Bought her, you mean. How'd she get here?"

"A rich tourist hired a mule to bring her to the

states and get her past immigration. She was probably about to be groomed. We got her just in time."

"Now what?"

"Friends International wants to arrange for a ticket back, but the D.A. won't release her because she's a witness to murder.

"And there's more. Channary's the sister of a local Cambodian legend. Her brother's in a gang that prowls the Mekong River. Evidently he ripped off a drug lord and became Robin Hood—and Santa Claus. He leaves money for poor families while they're sleeping, along with a written Buddhist prayer for enlightenment. They call him 'The Ghost'."

Conley wrote, closed his notepad, and stood.

"Detective Mazzarelli says you're looking to do some undercover work," she said. "Told me to ask you about the Paladin."

"Mazzarelli's got a big mouth."

"So, what is it? This Paladin?"

"You don't want to know."

"Maybe not, but I'll do anything to help. I've done undercover before."

"Right. An undercover social worker."

"Former Army Ranger and a black belt in judo, and I've got a masters in law enforcement. Care to compare resumes, Detective?"

"I'm impressed, but no thanks."

Channary was walking toward them, smoothing her dress, combing her hair.

Thompson's face hardened, and when she spoke her voice was hushed but powerful. "Here's some advice for you, Detective. You need my help. In fact, from what I can see, you need it badly."

Chapter 20

Saturday morning brought sunshine, but not warmth. Conley watched the Kendricks' mini-van pull into Ocean Park Municipal Marina, a crowded yard full of tired-looking fishing trawlers and lobster boats put up for winter. Kit and Leshawn strained against their seatbelts, necks stretched, eyes wide, peering through the van's windows.

Curious about the world.

Madie looked too, but her wrinkled brow showed inquisition mixed with concern. Brown-bottomed boats sat on jack stands. Weathered scows lay on their sides, as if they'd been lashed and scattered by a Nor'easter. Lloyd Kendricks maneuvered around potholes in the unpaved lot, breaking thin layers of ice that frosted dark puddles of slush.

Conley sat near the launch ramp in his BMW, motor running, a plume of exhaust growing from the tailpipe. Kendricks parked next to him and they stepped out of their cars onto frozen dirt. Madie cradled a picnic basket in the crook of her arm. They gathered near the water.

"Which one's yours, Lloyd?" Conley asked.

Kendricks pointed to a solitary lobster boat in the harbor that listed toward them as if longing for shore.

Conley whistled. The sorry-looking boat clung by a frayed line to a baby blue buoy. The bow had yellow streaks the color of egg yolk. A tarnished pulley wheel hung from the wheelhouse, its spool empty.

"Don't be judging me, Conley. I bought it for almost nothing."

"Looks like you almost paid what it's worth."

Kit looked at the boat and dropped his knapsack.

"We gonna swim to it?" he asked.

"We could," Conley said. "Let's take the rowboat instead and we'll pick everyone up at the pier. We got a rowboat, right, Lloyd?"

"'Course we do."

They passed an upside-down stack of small boats and stopped at a weather-beaten skiff. Its name—DESTINY—shone in bright letters on the stern, letters as white as cake frosting. They dragged the heavy boat to the launch ramp, scraping a shallow trench in the hardpack. Beautiful reds, blues, and purples swirled an oily welcome when the bottom met water. They found a single wooden oar near a pile of broken pallets and rusted drums. When the two of them stepped into the boat, a gob of gray putty popped from the floor and danced on a tiny blossom of water.

Kendricks stared at the puncture.

"That gonna hurt us much?" he asked.

Conley shrugged. "Water's on the wrong side of the boat, Lloyd."

Conley rowed with the one paddle, Indian style, and made his strokes longer and faster as the water inside deepened. His boots were soaked, feet already numb from the frigid water. The fast-filling rowboat barely moved from the one-oar stroke.

They reached the buoy and he fastened the prow ring quickly. He pulled himself into the lobster boat clumsily, hands slipping on the low wall. The salt air and countless coats of paint had made it as hard and greasy as a clamshell. Kendricks followed. The rowboat was a quarter full now, pulling the line to the buoy taut.

At the cockpit Kendricks reached under the steering wheel, retrieved a rusty key, and turned the ignition.

A faint whirr sounded, slowed, quieted.

"Who sold you this boat?" Conley asked.

Kendricks hesitated. "Louie the Lug. He needed bail money."

"Ever listen to the engine, Lloyd?"

"'Course I did. Sounded healthy. Loud and strong."

Kendricks turned the key again and after three weak chugs, the engine coughed to life and sent up a flag of white smoke from the stack pipe. Floorboards shook and a steady clang rang from the centerboard. A squeal escaped from somewhere under the deck.

"Bilge pump," Conley said.

"That's good, right? It's working hard."

"Working too hard, Lloyd. It needs a new bearing."

Madie and the boys stood at the end of the dock. Kendricks wiped his palm across his forehead.

"We going to pull this off, Conley?"

Conley looked toward the pier, then back at the buoy. The rowboat was almost underwater, only its outline visible, dark water covering the seats.

"Let's just get to the pier." He nodded at the rowboat. "We don't have much choice."

He nudged the throttle lever forward. The engine growled, speed dipping dangerously, smokestack spewing. The prop splashed behind them and the boat shuddered and lurched forward.

The Kendricks family was waiting, six eyes following every move.

"We take them around the harbor," Conley said, "and hug the shore in case we have to beach it."

Kendricks nodded. "Sounds like a plan."

Conley spun the ship's wheel and maxed the throttle. The boat turned drunkenly toward the pier. Madie frowned and hugged Kit with one arm. Kendricks hung on to the gunwale, knuckles as white as the ice clouding the windshield.

The boat slowed and eased into neutral. They drifted to the gray pier, toward Madie and the boys, frozen as statues.

"Take the wheel, Captain," Conley said to Kendricks as he checked frayed lines and faded pink bumpers, leaped onto the dock, and tied the boat to a cleat.

Kit put his hands on his knees and bent over to look at his father. "You the captain, Daddy?"

"He sure is," Conley said, planting his foot against the boat when a plastic bumper cracked like an eggshell and wood knocked against wood. "And I'm the mate."

"Daddy your boss?" Leshawn asked.

"Captain's everybody's boss," Kit said angrily.

Madie and the boys got into the boat.

"This boat's crooked, Lloyd," Madie said.

Conley led them to the port side of the deck—the high side—and had them sit on the weathered bench.

"I'll take over, Captain," he said and steered the boat toward the inlet that led to open ocean.

Kit peered past his father. "You letting your mate steer, Daddy?"

"Just a little."

Kendricks sat next to Madie, arm around her. The boys got brave and tried their sea legs, exploring the boat. Kit opened the wooden bait bin, smelled decades of fish heads, and closed it fast. He looked in the tiny cabin and saw the flapping door to the head.

"Can we sleep down there?"

"Sure," Conley called. "Just need to swab it first, clean the toilet maybe."

"Mate stuff, huh?"

He looked back at Kendricks and Madie, arm in arm on the bench. The harbor opening framed them, blue sky and bluer sea. Kendricks stared straight ahead, smiling as if he saw something that pleased him in the air.

"That's right," Conley said. "Mate stuff."

The engine clanged louder. He cut the speed and knelt next to the engine hold. He lifted the door on a creaky hinge and watched the vibrating Mercury engine. It was caked with dirt, spark plug cables cut and frayed. Brown water sloshed underneath.

Kendricks knelt next to him, hands on his knees.

"What's the problem, Conley?"

"Bad plug or cable if you're lucky. Bad piston if you're not."

"I vote for the plug and cable theory."

"We'll change them first, then do a compression check."

"We gonna sink?" Kit asked from the other side, hands on his knees like his dad.

"No way," Conley said. "Can't sink on a shakedown cruise."

"That's good. That water down there is pee-eew."

"Lloyd," Madie called. "Maybe we should go

back."

"What do you think, Conley?" he whispered.

"Smart lady. We're almost to the other side of the harbor. I nurse the engine and take it back to the marina dock. Worst case is tide goes out and you're grounded. These boats have big skegs that protect the prop."

"I like it."

He swung the boat across the harbor inlet, prayed it didn't quit near the foaming sea. They motored past the Ocean Park Yacht Club, home of gleaming pleasure boats and gaudy yachts. The pier in front had a fancy canvas cover.

The engine held, coughing, dieseling. He finally cut the motor and they drifted back to Gibbs Marina as if on a track. Kendricks grabbed the lines this time, jumped onto the dock, and tied off the boat the way Conley had.

Madie was already unpacking sandwiches and handing them out. Kit leaned over the side and started tearing pieces of bread and dropping them to minnows. Leshawn joined him.

"How bad a shape this boat in, Conley?" Kendricks whispered.

"Every boat needs something, and some boats need everything."

"I'm talking about this boat."

"I'd say this is one of the everything variety."

"Take a lot of money, won't it?"

"Yep. Unless you do it yourself."

Kendricks nodded. "I got a confession. I don't really know much about boats."

"Shocker."

Kendricks glanced at his family, folded his hands,

kneaded them. "Hey, Conley. I got a proposition for you. How'd you like to go in half on this boat? No cash. Your know-how and my git-up-and-go. Like an investment."

Conley looked at Madie and the boys. They were quietly eating now, staring at the glitzy boats across the harbor. The boys leaned into their mother like bookends. Lloyd didn't know boats, but he certainly knew families. Kendricks was blessed with something better than yachts and mansions. His family was his treasure.

Kendricks unlocked his hands and thrust his right one out hard, thumb up. Madie's gaze drifted toward them. Conley shook the hand.

A big cabin cruiser—a twin to his and Lisa's—left the yacht club and purred by. It left a wake that roiled the water around them and made the lobster boat seesaw and its gear shake. Suddenly the rusted pulley snapped and crashed. A tiny cloud of rust powdered the deck.

"We better start right away," he said as he watched the sleek boat clear the harbor and disappear into the horizon. "Cruising weather will be here before you know it."

Chapter 21

Channary slept fitfully, as usual. Night and day were reversed in this crazy land. In Cambodia, night was for sleeping. In America, everything happened in the darkest hours. Often she was awakened by the constant roar—cars, trucks, airplanes, the nearby factory—that she'd come to think of as the sound of America. Other times the boys in the house woke her. They were busiest at night—running, slamming doors, shouting orders to each other, even louder now, on the weekend.

She sat up in bed. Three other girls shared her room, but not her sleep problem. They enjoyed deep sleep, their breaths long and shallow. The dolls on their beds had dead, staring eyes, sparkling from the streetlight outside, that reminded her of friends at the orphanage. Were her friends waiting for her return? Or were they sad they'd never see her again?

She lay down and thought of her mother, begging in front of their tiny, worn shack. She'd point Channary out to passersby as she pleaded for money and food, and had taught her daughter to make a sad face Channary had feared would freeze forever.

The beating machines outside became a steady drone, and Channary's eyes wanted to close. She sighed deeply.

Conley, the kind policeman, stood on a porch and

beckoned her. Not a tenement porch like she was used to, but one on a pretty house like she'd seen in picture books. His handsome face smiled. A swing sat in the side yard, and a garden beyond. Sheila tended the garden plants, tall beyond belief, and brushed the soil from her hands and clothes. She climbed the steps to the porch and laced her fingers with Conley's, and together they called her.

"Channary, come. Channary—"

She awoke with a start and sat up straight. The bedroom door swung open and three of the Aunties hurried in, a finger to their mouths. Each lifted a girl, cradling them like babies. The women's hair smelled like soap, their breath like cinnamon. The other girls protested sleepily and were shushed. The Aunties closed the bedroom door behind them. Their long dresses whispered as they hurried down the hallway, Channary and the girls in their arms, and carefully descended the stairs.

****

Samay followed Vithu down a narrow alley to a one-story building whose peeling sign simply said LAUNDRY. Samay followed him inside. The floor was faded linoleum and the walls were scarred paneling. An overhead fan turned lazily. Somewhere in back, laundry presses hissed and workers chatted noisily. Samay rounded a counter whose Formica top was held together with tape, and sat on a stool behind a cash register

"Repeat your instructions," Vithu said.

"I wait for Ramon and let him in."

"And what do you say?"

"Nothing."

"And then?"

"When Ramon leaves, I follow."

Vithu turned the sign in the window to CLOSED and smiled. "You've found your perfect job, Samay—doing the three things you do best—wait, shut up, and follow."

Do what you do best, Vithu. Leave.

Samay's hate for his mentor seemed to grow daily, and he contemplated what do with the secret he held—that Vithu had started selling drugs against Pon's wishes.

After a long time, the rusted sleigh bells on the door signaled the arrival of Ramon, Diaz's friend from the Hispanic Club. He looked worn. Tan was fading, cheeks showing coins of pale skin. Goatee was ragged, eyes bloodshot.

"Where's Trong Tri?" Ramon asked.

Samay gathered the green curtain behind him and slid it along the aluminum tube. The wizened old man named Trong Tri sat on a thin mattress on a wooden slab. A wispy crown of white was all the hair he owned, save for an equally sparse mustache flecked with crumbs of bread. The man's eyes studied the delicate tea service on a stand in front of him. A poster of Vietnam decorated the wall behind, lush green gardens on a blond wall panel.

Ramon tapped the man's chin hard enough to clack yellow teeth together and make the mustache crumbs fly.

"Let's go, old man."

"No. I quit," he said. "Choose another."

Ramon smiled as he squatted, resting his arms on his quads, folding his hands.

"Cambodians, Trong Tri," he said, a delicious

whisper. "Cambodians. Sworn enemies of every Viet. A brave strike against them. An hour of your time. Translate what she says, that's all. Simple for you. You're a master of their silly gibberish."

Trong Tri's head started to shake.

"Choose another. Leave a tired old man." He pulled crisp bills out of the pocket of his baggy pants and offered them.

Ramon stood, unfolded his hands, and clapped them back together. He blew into the space between his thumbs.

"Sorry. You've been paid. There are no refunds in this life, my friend." He cocked his head. "Maybe in the next."

He lifted Trong Tri by one arm and signaled Samay to take the other. They dragged him out of his cubby, around the colorful counter, under the cheery chime of door bells. Arm in arm they passed shuttered, sleeping stores. Trong Tri cried as they pulled him down the alley, thin shoes scraping asphalt, loose clothes waving and flapping in protest. Plastic bags and rotten vegetables lined the way, an earthy stink that made the crowded Vietnamese section of Ocean Park smell like a farm. They passed tiny storefronts, buildings painted with splashes of outrageous color that distracted the eye from broken shingles, peeling paint, rusted drainpipes.

The back door of the van opened when they reached it. Five men sat on bench seats that lined the walls. One was striking, more a bull than a man, covered with black hair so flat and greasy it looked like a hide, and with arms the size of cannons, covered with sleeves of tattoos. Dark, merciless eyes darted like a lizard's. Where was this monster from?

Hell, maybe.

Ramon held the door wide, threw Trong Tri onto the van's floor, and bunched Samay's shirt in his fist.

"You saw nothing. You remember no one. Otherwise, you'll share the old man's fate. Got that?"

Samay nodded.

Ramon started the van and pulled away toward the river. Gray paint and dull tires, slightly tinted windows, stock as stock could be, forgettable as a gust of wind.

When they were out of sight, Samay ran to his scooter and followed.

****

Soon after, Samay shut off his motorbike and pushed it the length of River Street. He turned onto a dirt path and hid behind a high hedge that bordered the courtyard of the tenements. The van sat in a dark corner. Trong Tri could be heard inside, sobbing—until two sharp slaps rang. Silence followed.

The back door opened. Ramon and four Latin Kings jumped to the ground and scattered. One hid in the dark alcove formed by a porch, another under the awning of a side door. The third disappeared down the alley next to the tenement as Ramon and another gangbanger climbed the porch stairs. They twisted the unlocked doorknob and slipped inside.

Crickets chirped in the weeds along the bank behind Samay, and animals scurried through the weeds. The Saugus River murmured, fish splashed. The earthy stink of mud and vegetation filled his nostrils.

A creak came from the van, almost imperceptible. A grunt followed soon after from the direction of the first sentry, quick and low, then a cry from the second's position. Minutes passed before the van creaked gently again.

The silhouette of Ramon, unmistakable, burst from the tenement's entrance, leaped down the steps, and sprinted across the courtyard. Samay positioned his kick starter. The back door of the van opened slowly and Trong Tri crouched on the lip, holding the door open like wings.

"Go, go, go," Ramon yelled. "Close the damn door, old man."

Trong Tri's hand snaked out from the blackness, circled Ramon's neck, and yanked him inside. Samay pulled down his ski mask, kicked his bike to life, sped to the van, and looked within. The bull was turned to the wall, his muscled back still. Trong Tri was sitting on Ramon, knees pinning his arms in crucifixion.

The feeble Trong Tri had become Pon again. His mustache was gone and his scalp was flecked with blood. The moon lit the tiny, angry pink replica of itself on his chin, the half-inch crescent scar. His skin seemed tighter, younger, as if he'd found the fountain of youth here on the banks of the foul-smelling Saugus River. His hand flashed behind him, drew a serrated knife, and held it close to Ramon's face.

"Don't kill me," Ramon begged.

Pon dragged his fingertips lightly across Ramon's handsome cheek. "I won't, my friend. But maybe you'll wish I had."

"Anything. I'll do anything," Ramon cried, not so tough now that he wasn't beating an old man.

"Good. You will bring a message."

"What do I say?"

"Nothing. You say nothing."

Pon's hand hid Ramon's eyes like a blindfold and

clamped his head still. Ramon bellowed, and his cry swirled around the van's metal walls and echoed with a metallic twang as Pon sliced one side of Ramon's face from mouth to ear, then the other. Ramon choked, gargled, and groaned. He'd been given the widest, wettest smile in the world.

"No more beauty in this life," Pon said, then jumped out and straddled the back of Samay's scooter.

"Maybe in the next," Pon yelled before they sped away.

Chapter 22

Ocean Park didn't have enough ambulances to carry all the dead. One from Saugus arrived, slowing when it neared swirling blue lights. Police tape formed bright yellow fences that made cattle pens for the chattering neighbors. A news van followed the ambulance and tried to tailgate past the police checkpoint. Uniformed cops banged fists on the side of the van, cursed the reporters, ordered them off the street.

Conley stood next to a makeshift wall of wooden poles and black plastic that hid the bodies in the front yard. His heart still pounded a drumbeat that had begun when the call came in. He'd raced to her house, a ride he couldn't even remember now, and his pounding heart didn't slow until he saw Channary unharmed, felt the pulse in her tiny, warm hand, and led her to the safety of a neighbor.

Stefanos arrived and grabbed the collars of two young local cops, pulled their faces close to his, told them to guard the neighbor's front and back doors with their lives. "And shoot to kill," he screamed, the veins on the back of his hands as blue as the bunched uniforms he held.

Crime scene techs shuttled between the bodies on the ground. The corpse nearest the street was a rag doll. Hispanic male in his twenties, strong build, dressed in black. Dressed for death. Stefanos squatted and spoke to the dead man.

"Hope it hurt, asshole—a lot."

Mazzarelli had just arrived. His hair was disheveled and his slack tie hung like a paisley noose.

"You okay, Captain?"

Stefanos rose and smoothed the wrinkles from his pants. "About time you showed up. Take notes."

Mazzarelli straightened and dug a notepad and pencil stub out of his overcoat pocket.

The three of them walked to the corpse in the alley.

"Another Hispanic," Stefanos said. "Latin Kings probably. Somebody gutted them both from belly to neck."

Conley, Stefanos, and Mazzarelli climbed the steps of the three-family house, past the officer holding the logbook, to the victim on the second floor landing. He was curled into a ball, dead hands clutching his chest, dark hat shading lifeless eyes.

"Last two were edged-weapon attacks," Stefanos said. He knelt on one knee. "Cuts have a bevel to them, probably came from behind. Angled strikes."

Conley remembered a coroner saying knife wounds were agonizing—thousands of nerves screaming, thousands of points of pain.

A patrolman approached and whispered to Stefanos.

"Captain, we got enough meat wagons now. Techs need to do their work."

"Ten minutes."

They climbed to the third floor, Mazzarelli wheezing and glistening with sweat. They inspected the hallway and bedrooms. Spartan spaces—mattress and a chair, clothes in piles against the wall. They walked into Channary's bedroom and stood over the body on the floor. This gangbanger looked like a teenager.

"Scrimmage wounds," Stefanos said as Mazzarelli wrote with a tiny pencil, tongue out, eyes straining. "Lunging stabs from the front, knife twists to open a hole as big as a baseball. Killed quietly. Quiet and sure."

"Dark clothes again," Conley said. "Like commandos, all except for the one in the van. They placed lookouts. This was well-planned."

Mazzarelli wrote fast, big hands pinching the pencil. He flipped a page and spoke.

"Buddy D'Amico's the stiff in the van, Captain. He was just two weeks out of Cedar Junction. Child molesters like Buddy usually don't do too good in that pit, but he'd managed all right. Raped most every guy under thirty, but none of them would testify. Hard to imagine someone could strangle a guy with a neck like that."

"Thank God someone did."

Conley visited the rooms again, and the second floor landing. The perps had numbers and lookouts.

So how'd they get ambushed?

Outside, a reporter held a microphone in front of a statuesque redhead in the middle of the street. A crowd gathered around them. Conley strained to see.

Lisa.

Human misery attracted politicians as well as media. His wife the candidate held court, pointing at the death house, eyes shifting from one listener to another, a calculated second and a half, just enough to form a bond, maybe grab a vote.

He knew the spiel. Safer streets. Better-trained police. Programs. Money. He'd heard it a million times. Simple solutions. Everything was easy for those who didn't have to do it.

"Kendricks just arrived," Mazzarelli said to Stefanos.

"Tell him to take a look at this mess, then see me."

"A drug beef, Captain?"

"I don't think so."

Outside, more reporters strained against the police tape and shouted questions at stone-faced policemen.

"This'll get national coverage," Mazzarelli said. "Local businessman's death gets local newspaper's front page. Drug dealer gets the metro section. Massacres get network news specials. News vultures must have all the rules written down in a book somewhere. We got a motive, Captain?"

He nodded upstairs. "They wanted Channary."

"The girl in the church?"

"The last intruder was in her bedroom—farthest one from the van. Thank God she wasn't there." He dug a fist into his palm and turned to Conley. "Time to get to work, Detective. The Latin Kings have targeted our Channary."

****

An ambulance left with the last body after noon. Conley and Stefanos joined Channary in the neighbor's house. Conley sat next to her on a musty couch and Stefanos sat in a wingchair. The coffee table between them was cluttered with religious pictures and statues of saints.

Channary and the saints—a team of innocents.

She clutched a blond doll and caressed its limp

hair.

"Hello, Channary," Stefanos said.

"Hello, sirs, and good afternoon."

"Your English is improving."

"Yes," she said, smiling. "Sheila knows many words."

"I bet she does. Do you know what happened last night?"

"No."

Channary caressed the doll's straw hair harder and smoothed it closer to its head.

"Did you hear noise?" he asked. "Voices?"

"The trees whispered good night to me. They always do. And then I slept with the Aunties last night."

"I see. Nothing else?"

"The trees had nothing else to say."

"Do you remember Kendricks and Conley?"

"Sheila says Kendricks is funny and Conley is handsome."

"Do you like them?"

Her face turned red. "Yes."

Kendricks walked in the front door, arguing loudly with the patrolmen posted guard. One pinned him to the wall before Conley refereed. Still breathing hard from the tussle, Kendricks sat on the sofa, and Channary smiled that beautiful lazy crescent of perfect, salmon-colored lips and teeth the color of pearls.

Conley placed his arm around her.

Stefanos sat back and folded his hands.

"I'm glad you like them, Channary, because you'll be staying together for a while."

Chapter 23

Conley, Kendricks, and Channary left River Street and drove to Nahant, a hilly patch of vacation houses, an eclectic mix of historic homes and contemporary retreats slammed onto every spit of available land. Nahant tried like hell to be an island, but the two-mile causeway that connected Ocean Park forced it to be a peninsula. Overachievers lived in the tiny bedroom community, and the local cops always rousted Ocean Park kids to make sure the privileged kept their status.

Channary rode in Kendricks' sedan, lost in the expansive back seat. She pulled herself to the window and pointed at the beach and its pounding waves.

"Atlantic," she said to Conley, proud she remembered the word. "The shining sea."

They turned onto the main road, a winding climb that lifted them past houses clinging to slopes. The glimmering Boston skyline in the distance seemed close enough to touch.

The safe house sat hidden at the end of a tree-lined dead-end street. Its small backyard dropped off to a steep cliff, topped by a chain link fence.

Conley and Kendricks stopped beside a Nahant police cruiser at the beginning of the street under a big maple.

"You the only one?" Kendricks said to the young cop behind the wheel.

"Don't sweat, Detective," the cop said, "We keep this town pretty damn secure. We're small though, can't afford to dedicate a lot of patrolmen to sit in cars all day. Besides, this street's well-protected and that house has more alarms than Fort Knox."

Kendricks and Conley parked in the driveway and unloaded bags from the trunk. Channary rolled an old-fashioned hard suitcase past a new kitchen, a wide-screen TV, and modern furniture that looked out of place in the antique home.

Kendricks hefted his bag onto the couch, unzipped the side compartment, and set family pictures on end tables.

Conley looked up the stairway to total darkness. They chose bedrooms and unpacked. Dusk was approaching, and a stillness came over the neighborhood, despite the distant roar of surf. Suddenly footsteps clattered on the front stairs. Kendricks drew his gun. Conley approached the door slowly and watched silhouettes behind the thin shears. A hooker appeared to be arguing with their sentry. Safe neighborhood indeed. Three knocks were followed by a fourth. He opened the door cautiously.

Thompson stood next to a blushing Nahant cop. She was transformed. Her dress fit like a tight black leather glove, its low neckline showed an acre of skin, and stiletto heels made her long legs seem even longer.

She cocked her hip and threw her head back.

"Ready for our date, Conley?"

Kendricks holstered his gun. "Captain says this is dangerous. Besides, he says there is no Paladin."

"Perfect," she said. "Tell your captain if there's no Paladin, there's no danger. I'll be in the car."

Kendricks looked past her. "Tell him yourself. There's him and Mazzarelli, coming to visit." He sat back on the couch and nodded at Sheila. "You got your hands full there, Conley."

Conley grabbed his coat to follow her down the steps. "Don't wait up. No telling when I'll be back." He grinned. "Hopefully never."

****

At midnight, Channary cracked open the bedroom window, and the salty air that seeped in from the ocean seemed to give the bed sheets weight and make them smell smoky, like fresh sails. She snuggled in the covers and felt sleep coming. Time to dream, but hard to fall asleep with all the noise. Loud waves crashed outside. A motorboat roared far away.

She smiled and yawned. Her eyes began to close.

The house again. The swing on the porch was still, and the garden plants swayed in the breeze. She climbed the steps and looked inside. She'd never made it this far. Where were Conley and Sheila? She ran to the garden and searched.

Someone called from the house and she ran inside again. A man stood in the sun-baked hallway. His eyes were black marbles, his white lips pressed together tightly, and blood moved down his handsome suit like a living thing.

She woke with a start, screaming, and when Captain Stefanos came running she held onto him with all her might.

Chapter 24

Father McCarrick was not happy. Monday was his day to sleep late, but the growl of a diesel engine woke him early. He curled his bedroom window shade back with a finger. A news van was parked out front, its lazy-looking driver puffing smoke out the crack of an open window. Needed a shave, McCarrick could tell from here. He had a mind to call the police if that's all Smokey was going to do, loiter and despoil the environment. The driver had already flipped three butts onto Summer Street.

Another truck pulled up behind, this one with the ungrateful Jewish girl, still scratching that jet-black mop of hers. Bugs, probably.

Two more vans. Men drifted out and slammed car doors, explosions in the early morning stillness. They were in no hurry to approach the Jew. Couldn't blame them—head lice were highly contagious.

Disappointing really. If this was all St. Ambrose's had drawn, small fleet of rusted white vans with rainbow-colored letters of local news stations—

Wait. The newcomers turned to the sound of rolling thunder, and stared down Summer Street. A behemoth crept toward them. A gigantic truck, gray dishes sitting on its rooftop, giant salad bowls aimed at heaven. No four-letter W call letters on this monster. A Network. The big time. Three familiar letters graced the side of the van, large and proud. Damn the Olympics, Super Bowls, Hollywood murder trials. The Church of St. Ambrose was center stage today, and its story required satellites.

Movement on the left. Father Spinelli stood in the driveway, hand shading eyes from the sun, tight curls rising from the back of his hairy paw. He headed toward the trucks.

McCarrick ran downstairs, twisted the knob on the rectory front door, and threw it open.

Father Spinelli was standing in front of the church, arms spread like Christ the Redeemer.

"The church is closed, ladies and gentlemen. Schedule of Masses is on the sign. Confessions are on Saturday."

Not a very welcoming Redeemer.

"Why is it closed?" Debbie Feldman asked, drawing out the word 'closed' as if only she knew how to pronounce it. "What are you hiding, Father?"

Microphones blossomed and others joined in, slowly advancing.

"Is the statue still crying?"

"Has the Vatican been notified?"

They stepped forward and Spinelli shuffled back, arms outstretched as if he could somehow contain the crowd.

McCarrick strode across the lawn between them and joined Spinelli.

"This is public property," a gray-haired man with a tie said, loud and clear. "Taxpayers paid for this church."

Father Spinelli lowered his hands and cupped them in front of him as if he were holding an infant.

"Taxpayers? No they didn't. Parishioners paid for the church, along with The Holy See—"

"He's right," McCarrick bellowed in his best Sunday-sermon voice. "St. Ambrose's is a church of the people."

"What the hell does that mean?" Father Spinelli sputtered.

"Just go with it," McCarrick muttered. "Who knows who paid for the church, Frank? Happened a hundred years ago, for Christ's sake. This is television. Truth is irrelevant."

A man in jeans and a parka ran around them and tried the front door. Locked.

"The door is locked," Father Spinelli said. "Don't bother trying."

Mrs. Blodgett suddenly appeared. "Father Spinelli, you just have to jiggle the knob. Lock's broken, remember?"

McCarrick smiled as the crowd surged past the priests, yanked the door open, and jostled to get inside. Most looked like laborers—hairy, unkempt. A few were well dressed—two men, one woman—their arms held high against the crowd, a clever maneuver to guard perfect hair and stretch handsome suits and dress so they wouldn't wrinkle.

They poured inside, equipment knocking against ancient doorframes and pews. They shouted, barked orders, and smoked cigarettes in the cold, dry church. Debbie Feldman led the irreverent army to the Madonna and they dropped equipment on the floor. Two of them leaned back against the communion rail, fat asses resting on the red leather. One dabbed his cigarette butt in a votive candle.

The priests were close behind, a noisy caboose.

"This is private property," Father Spinelli yelled to the crowd.

"Not really, Frank."

"Yes, it is."

"No, it isn't."

"I'm not going to argue with you."

"Certainly sounds like arguing to me, Frank."

Mrs. Blodgett held the door, unable to step inside. Thick black cables were being dragged into St. Ambrose's from the big van. They coiled, curled, and straightened like striking snakes, whipsawed the gritty floor, hissed as they slid. She waited patiently and stepped lively through the entrance when the wires finally stilled.

Blinding light shone on the Madonna. A technician had found an electrical outlet, plugged in, and turned a bleaching bulb on the Blessed Mother. Mary didn't look so good. The cracks in her face looked like wrinkles. They even laced her pink and blue robe.

Father Spinelli searched the side altar, found the plug, and pulled. That light died, but another came to life instantly. He scrambled to find the outlet and stubbed his foot on the pedestal under the statue.

A news anchor shrugged himself ready. Cameras rolled. Polished speech filled the church.

Father McCarrick folded his arms and turned to his housekeeper. His deliberate murmur seemed unnecessary given the hubbub.

"Lots of activity."

"Yes, Father."

"We need to support St. Ambrose's."

"Yes, Father."

"Are you prepared?"

"I am."

A skinny blonde holding a microphone waved a bony hand at McCarrick. He waved back, and she crooked her finger and beckoned him.

He shot his cuffs and squared his shoulders.

"Then get back to the kitchen and do your magic, Mrs. Blodgett. They look like a hungry bunch."

Chapter 25

Sheila Thompson nuzzled the side of Conley's neck, her warm breath caressing him. He raised his chin to savor the smoothness. Her soft hair fell across his face. He closed his eyes in mock rapture. After all, they were…

Pretending.

He slid his hand down her supple back and let it rest on the rise of her hips. She was graceful as a ballerina, swaying as she ground against him. Hard to believe they were…

Acting.

Their disguises—she'd dyed her hair red and he'd grown a goatee—made him feel like they were strangers who'd just met, even on this third night posing as a couple hunting for the Paladin, the sex club that had threatened Victor Rodriguez. Third night—a Monday—trolling the sleaziest Boston couples bars they could find. Other couples danced toward them, spinning and drifting away like saucers in a teacup ride. The mirrored ball in Misty's Tavern painted them with colored light.

The music stopped. They walked away from the dance floor and sat at a small table to wait for new couples. New propositions. She swirled merlot in her glass and watched the red tears run down the inside.

Thompson had a lot in common with Conley's wife

Lisa. Women of resolve, both of them used to getting their way.

So very determined.

Lisa and Sheila Thompson—*the same.*

But Lisa was all about career and Thompson would go to the wall for an abandoned little girl she barely knew.

So very different.

When it came to warfare, Lisa was the German army—and Sheila Thompson the Russian winter.

The gauntlet began.

Big Hair made the first run. Her mate trailed behind, a young dude with a jet-black mullet.

"Hey, you guys are new," she said and thrust her breasts so far forward her halter top became transparent. She placed a hand on the back of Thompson's chair.

"Only to you." Thompson smiled, covering the hand with her own.

"Looking to party?" Mullet said in a voice so low Conley felt it in his chest.

"Sure," Thompson said. "Let's head for the Paladin."

"Never heard of it," the woman murmured and massaged Thompson's arm and shoulders. "How's a hot tub sound?"

"You know what?" Thompson said, shrugging the hand away. "We're not interested after all."

Cold wind howling across the Siberian tundra, so powerful it drives powdered snow back toward the sky.

Who would have guessed?

The couple stormed away.

The waitress approached for the third time in

minutes. Persistent. Young. Plain black skirt. White dress shirt. Look-away eyes. Conley held his hand over his glass. Thompson shook her head. The girl hesitated, turned, and left.

A young blonde approached next, golden-haired like a Nordic princess. The body builder at her side did the talking.

"Hey," he said.

Eloquent.

Thompson ran her hand along his rippling arm. "Sit down, handsome."

The blonde was quiet as she took the seat next to Conley and pressed her thigh against his. Muscles sat next to Thompson and she stroked his arm as if he were a pet. He swung his face toward hers.

"We were just getting ready to leave. How about you?"

"Sure. Ever hear of the Paladin?"

"No."

Thompson pulled her hands away as if they'd been burned, and leaned back in her seat.

"Buzz off," she said and sipped wine. "Amateur."

Vast, quiet steppes covered by cracked ice that looked like broken mirrors. Bare, bent trees that nature seemed to have forgotten.

Waitress was back, a nuisance.

Nothing was going right and time was wasting. Maybe the Paladin never existed. Maybe William had it all wrong. Maybe Sage was a liar.

"We wait," Thompson said, and it was as if she had read his mind. "We wait because that's what always works, doesn't it? All things come to she who waits."

He lifted his beer. "To those who wait," he

corrected.

She smiled. He tried not to, but he couldn't help but smile back.

The waitress set a cocktail napkin in front of him along with a beer he hadn't asked for. She set a full glass of wine next to the almost-full one Thompson held. The girl laid a business card in front of him and snapped the corner with her thumbnail before she left. A telephone number was scrawled on the back.

He turned the card over and looked up. The waitress was gone.

"Congratulations," Thompson said. "Lucky stiff, Conley. You got a date. Maybe you didn't need me after all."

He shook his head and showed the card to her. A wide border of scrolls and curlicues—red, purple, orange—surrounded bold letters that spelled a name—THE PALADIN.

Chapter 26

Conley called the number on the card and jotted down the address of the Paladin. Thompson set her Mercedes' GPS and they headed toward Boston. They crossed the Mystic River Bridge and drove toward the lighted skyline that blazed in a muted winter glow. They negotiated the narrow streets of the North End and financial district until they were at warehouses on the shorefront. Cars lined every available street parking space, and it took them fifteen minutes to find an open spot. Thompson parked and Conley phoned in their position. They walked the dark waterfront in silence, footsteps echoing, until they stopped.

Three curved steps extended from a windowless building like an open hand, a building that matched Sage's sketch. A dull aluminum rail split the stairway and led to a door covered with riveted metal plates. The front of the place was a sheer wall, a red-brick cliff. No street number on the door. No sign. Just a curved coil of green tubing over the entrance that led to a plain fixture with a stingy bulb.

The alley was quiet, a dead-end valley surrounded by man-made mountains of mortar and clay. Conley stepped on the first stair and the building seemed to hum a slow rush, a dull heartbeat.

"You sure this is the Paladin?" Thompson asked.

"Looks like it." *It has to be.* "Ready?" He clasped

the frigid rail.

She gave him an arch look and walked past him to the door. Determined. Fearless.

"Wait," he said, and pulled a wad of paper from his pocket, unfolded it on his open hand, and smoothed it with the other. "Take a last look at Carrie."

She stood next to him, shoulders touching, and they studied the drawing. Carrie's chin tilted down and her lifeless hair framed a frightened face. Eyes peered from under furrowed brows. Her name was written at the bottom of the page in flowing letters. Funny how a name under a picture gave it soul.

"We talk to Carrie and no one else," he said. "Sage says to trust her."

He stared at the portrait and kept smoothing the page even after it was flat. When he saw Carrie, he'd know, and not just from high cheekbones and a delicate chin. Sage had captured abject hopelessness in the woman's eyes.

He looked up. The hum grew loud. Music blared.

Thompson had opened the door and was stepping inside with one long-legged stride, one stilettoed step.

He pocketed the drawing, climbed the steps, grasped the round knob, held the door.

Abandon hope, all ye who enter.

****

The Paladin door closed with a bang. A huge, warehouse-size room stretched in front of him, a room of towering metal girders and concrete walls. Tiny spotlights glowed in the tall ceiling, lights that appeared as distant as stars and lit the perimeter of the room like a halo.

People danced in the center—shifting shapes that

billowed like black clouds in the dusk. Thompson was already far ahead, halfway around the room, making sure she was seen. He let her go. She'd more than proven her ability to take care of herself these past few nights.

The song ended. Dancers left the floor and blocked Conley's way. He studied them, searching for Carrie. Odd task, trying to compare flesh, blood, and hair with Sage's pencil sketches. He recognized one couple, but couldn't remember the names Sage had written under their portraits.

A young brunette next—*Mary? Marie?*

Marcie, that was it. And *Peter,* thin face and smiling lips, was right behind.

One by one, Sage's pencil people came alive and blossomed into three dimensions.

Toni stepped away from the crowd, dancing a slow grind with someone who was not her husband *Dan.*

Linda drank wine from a fluted glass. When it was finished, she turned and scooped a new one from a tray.

Artie's eyes darted around the floor, inspecting female bodies as if they were cattle.

Conley walked past, through a mix of perfume, cologne, and booze so pungent it seemed to wet the air, and he saw Carrie. She looked as tired as her picture, eyes narrowed to slits, hair tousled as if she'd just woken. He trapped her in a corner. She tried to pass.

"Carrie," he said. "Sage sent me."

Sage's picture of her was spot on. The upturned face spoke resignation and failure. Pupils were dilated and words slurred.

"Yeah?" she said dreamily, tilting her head. "Sage?"

"She said you'd help me find Victor's killer."

"Victor's dead? Bummer. You a cop?"

"Hell, no."

"Then why do you care?"

"He owed me money."

That, she understood.

Thompson had made it to the other side of the dance floor. He signaled her.

"Someone in the Paladin threatened Victor. Do you know who?"

Carrie closed her eyes and knit her brow. "I remember. It wasn't us. Victor came with a friend—Richard—and they argued. He threatened to kill Victor, not us. They had a big blowout, Liam was pissed."

Liam. Sage had thought him important enough to bring his picture to Conley's boat, and her voice had quavered when she spoke his name. *He gets what he wants, doesn't take no for an answer. He's rough with the girls sometimes—the willing and the unwilling.*

Carrie whispered conspiratorially. "Then this Richard dude fucked up. He said his last name, like he thought he was somebody important, or better than us. Said we better remember that name. *Drewits.* Like screw it, only with an s at the end." She gave a drug-induced giggle. "Only he was the one screwing up. We don't use last names in the Paladin. That's the number one rule."

Suddenly Conley spotted Liam at the other end of the hall, no mistaking him—strong jaw and feral eyes, just like the sketch. He was stalking Thompson, approaching her like prey. When he caught up to her he slid his thick arm around her shoulder and all but forced her through a red door.

Conley started toward them, but Carrie held his wrist. "Where you going, handsome? We just met."

"I'll be back."

Conley shouldered his way through the crowd. They'd become an amorphous shape, a single, human obstacle of flesh and bone. He fought past and followed through the red door. Small points of light flickered in a hallway ceiling like fireflies. Doors on both sides stretched ahead endlessly. He opened the first. Empty— except for mattresses on the floor, covered in silk sheets. He stopped and listened. The music from the dance room was muffled, but its percussion beat an eerie warning—*like war drums*. A woman's laughter erupted behind one door, long, deep moans rose from another. He threw one open.

Naked bodies writhed like a nest of snakes. Bodies—white, brown, and black—slithered on mattresses as if oiled. Sighs rose from the tangle, throaty laughs, labored breaths. A girl caressed his leg and he pulled away.

Back to the hallway. Too much time had passed. He called Thompson's name, and a door rattled ahead and an unmistakable voice rang out.

"Matt!"

He yanked the door open and stepped inside. She and Liam stood alone, facing each other like boxers. Her arms sported finger bruises and blood ran from the corner of her red lips. Liam was shirtless, covered in muscle and bulging blue veins—*blue rivers*—that crisscrossed his torso like chainmail over hard plates of flesh. His hands hung at his sides and his thick fingers looked strong as grappling hooks.

"Let's go," Conley told Thompson.

Liam's eyes narrowed as his jaw stiffened. "She's mine. Wait your turn."

"The lady came with me."

Liam's fist shot forward like a battering ram and smashed Conley in the nose. A split second later he'd pinned Conley to the wall with a forearm. Eyes as cold as death he leaned forward and spoke again, his inhuman breath warm as steam."I said fuck off."

Conley threw a few roundhouse punches into a steel-barreled chest. Thompson jumped the bastard from behind and went for the choke hold but he slipped out of it and threw her off. A kick between his legs brought only a grunt and a hiss. Still, when Conley hooked his ankle around Liam's calf and pushed off the wall as hard as he could, all three of them collapsed on the mattress, limbs motoring, breath heaving.

Thompson wriggled free, found the wall switch, and flicked the lights off. Conley rolled away and Liam searched for him in the dark, roaring curses.

"Now!" Conley shouted, slipping out of his jacket when Liam's strong paws caught a sleeve. Thompson yanked open the door and they darted into the big hall, into the din, louder now, walls beating faster, into the mob of dancers. They fought through arms, legs, and bodies, eager to exit the front door they'd searched so long to find. Outside, Conley saw Thompson had shucked her shoes.

He opened his mouth to speak, but she only shook her head and waved him off, then bolted off the doorstep and into a sprint through the valley of buildings. Conley followed, running as fast as he could, until behind them the insistent, infernal drumbeat became silent.

Chapter 27

The next morning, Stacia Drewicz smiled a wall of yellow teeth at Conley. It hadn't taken him long to isolate the correct spelling for the name Carrie had given him at the Paladin. Good old Richard's file had then provided more than enough reason to warrant a personal visit.

The woman's mustard-colored eyes darted playfully between him and Kendricks as she spoke, making Conley's breakfast sandwich roll over in his stomach. Was she actually flirting with them?

"Richard never married," she tittered. "God knows the girls were always after him, ever since grade school. But he was too busy with hobbies—computers, sailing toy ships in the pond, science fiction books. Never had time to find a girl and get serious."

Her pudgy hands fluttered as she spoke, holding still only for the words she stretched. Fat fingers flicked the air when she talked about her son's gadgets. Machines—such a silly fad. Her hands straightened, palms out and waving in a slow circle, polishing the space in front of her when she talked about Richard's missed romantic opportunities.

Conley slid back on the hard, slippery Victorian couch, and listened with as much patience as he could muster. He opened the folder on his lap—Richard Drewicz's arrest jacket.

No time for girls, Mrs. D? Richard had time enough for trouble. Hacked into a bank's computer, drew two years' probation from a soft judge. Then he beat a child pornography rap when his jpeg files magically self-erased. He had time for all that.

Movement on the right, outside her living room window. Blue uniforms blurred by white lace curtains. The Salem cops who'd brought the detectives leaned against their cruisers.

Footsteps overhead. *Richard?* Conley looked at the spot she studied on the ceiling.

"We need to speak with your son," he said, interrupting.

"He'll be down soon enough," she said. "What's this about?"

"Richard's name came up during the Victor Rodriguez murder investigation."

She chuckled, a grin so wide that it shut her jaundiced eyes and made her jowls shake.

"This is no joke, ma'am," Kendricks said.

A door creaked shut somewhere in the house, barely perceptible.

"I'm sorry, Officer, but the idea Richard knows anything about murder is ludicrous. He's not a very physical creature, you know—"

A creature.

"Technology and the arts, Detective. Those are Richard's passions. He and his friends are very artistic—"

Muffled sounds, the sweep of footsteps on carpeted stairs. Conley glanced at the main stairway—empty.

"Gentlemen, Richard can't help you," she said, leaning forward, eyes closed, head shaking. Her high, quivering hair formed a sweeping silver swirl like a giant seashell. Her flowered dress stretched over shoulders and bust.

Conley stood and walked to the foyer.

"Officer," Mrs. Drewicz called from behind, loud and shrill. The springs in her chair complained. She pointed a chubby finger at the floor. "Sit down. Right now. This is my house and I don't allow strangers to run roughshod through it."

He pushed the swinging door to the kitchen, just enough to see through.

A man stood on the last step of a narrow back stairway. Skinny. Receding hairline and wide eyes that made his head look like a small animal's. Baggy sweatpants and a T-shirt draped straight down from bony shoulders and arched back.

He stepped onto the kitchen floor gingerly, as if untrusting of the tiles. He crossed the kitchen and eased open a four-panel door that led to a basement. A light clicked on. An unpainted banister was on the right, and as Richard held it, his legs rose and felt for each step like an insect's.

Conley crossed the kitchen, the sound of his footsteps masked by that of Kendricks and Mrs. Drewicz arguing loudly.

"Probable cause, Mrs. Drewicz..."

"Police brutality...my lawyer..."

The stairs were rough, splintered slabs, narrow treads and high risers. Conley steadied himself on the banister and descended.

What's down there, Richard? What are you going to show me?

He brushed against the rough plaster wall and it

rained white powder. He paused at the bottom and looked around the corner.

Wires, pipes, and thick beams crisscrossed the low ceiling. The gray floor was a bed of ash. Cardboard boxes stood in piles against walls, tilting dangerously. Washer and dryer rested in a corner on wooden pallets. An oil furnace sat under a grimy window, rusty and old, like salvage from the ocean floor.

To his right was the only bright thing. An upright safe stood at the foot of the steps, a man-high, kelly-green metal box with PREMIER painted in gold letters over a combination wheel. He ran his hand over the smooth, cold front.

A strip of light shone under a flat door to a makeshift room of plywood and studs. Small sounds came from inside, the click and scuff of plastic.

Conley listened at the door. More noise—fast ticks, loud whimpering. Richard was inside. Conley tried the knob. Locked.

Movement on his right, very close. He turned quickly and felt a wash of warm breath.

"What's going on?" Kendricks asked, his face inches away.

The whimpering stopped.

He hears us.

"Why are you here, Lloyd?" Conley whispered. "Where's Mrs. Drewicz?"

"Upstairs. Madder'n hell and twice as noisy. Thought you might need backup."

Shuffling inside the room. The acrid smell of gasoline filled the damp air.

"Richard Drewicz," Conley called, banging a fist on the door. "Police. Open up."

The smell grew stronger. Conley stepped back and gave the door a kick that made the jamb shudder. Whirrs and clicks suddenly sounded behind them. He turned.

Mrs. Drewicz stood hunched at the safe, pink slippers painted with the gray ash from the floor. She spun the combination lock and worked the silver lever like a pump handle.

He kicked the door again and the frame splintered. Richard stood beside a pyre of plastic jewel cases, a red gas can in one hand, silver lighter in the other. The room reeked of gasoline. He held the lighter to the pyramid, punching it forward as he thumbed the spark roller.

Shots.

Bullets rang, pinging off metal, and thwacked into wood. Kendricks hit the floor and cursed, clutching his thigh.

Mrs. Drewicz stood poised at the open safe, the butt of a .22 rifle buried in the crook of her shoulder. Hands were steady, feet spread for balance, yellow eyes narrowed to dull ellipses, feral spheres.

Conley crouched, drew his automatic, and fired. Three quick pulls of the trigger, three bullets into her ample torso. Her dress fluttered and she fell back, propped upright by the open safe door.

Richard screamed and ran to her. Conley tore the lighter from his hand and kicked the .22 away.

Voices called from the kitchen.

"Man down," Conley yelled and knelt next to his partner.

"Told you she was mad," Kendricks said.

Footsteps clattered. Mrs. Drewicz's body was

blocking the stairs. The Salem cops rocked the big steel panel, and her lifeless body swayed back and forth. Richard clung to her, sobbing, until they finally caved forward and the safe door clanged shut.

Conley ripped Kendricks' pants leg away. Not much blood, and Kendricks was already trying to stand. A cop pushed him back down and opened a first aid kit.

Conley collected DVD jewel cases scattered on the floor. Names in jagged black ink marred their surface. There were so *many*. The name Chrissy was scrawled on one. Megan on another. More names. All girls.

More.

Matt was afraid he already knew the secret.

****

Late that afternoon, Conley's phone rang. Mazzarelli had good news. Mrs. Drewicz's bullet had taken a chunk of flesh from Kendrick's leg and it hurt like hell, but he'd be home in a day or two, good as new.

Sheila Thompson sat next to Conley in front of a computer screen at the Salem Police station. Richard Drewicz's DVDs made a small tower on the desk. Conley chose one and opened the case. Sheila stared at the blank screen as he loaded the disk.

The sound of ringing phones and serious voices drifted through the thin walls. Aromatic steam rose from strong coffee in the mugs they held, a small comfort.

"I'm scared, Conley."

"So am I." He pressed PLAY.

A date appeared—two years ago—across a picture of Mrs. Drewicz's living room. Blinds were closed, but bright light shone on a man on the couch. He casually read a magazine, then snapped his head to the right to the sound of young voices. Two children appeared, tow-headed little girls in summer dresses.

Thompson groaned.

Conley's hand nearly crushed the remote.

They studied the actors, searching for clues—and watching unspeakable acts. Was Channary in that pile of plastic? Would they see her next? Or the time after?

Tears welled in Thompson's eyes and wet her cheeks. Conley fast-forwarded the disc. Forensics would analyze these later, identify these monsters, and rescue the innocents. But right now they needed to find a clue, a connection, a link to the murder of Victor Rodriguez.

For the next three hours, Conley loaded one DVD after another in the computer drive. Images played in front of them—dark, vile tableaus.

An unexpected man appeared. They watched in silence, faces ashen. A motel. A steady camera. The still eye captured monstrous evil, children in the silk folds of white sheets, a smiling gargoyle between them, touching, caressing.

The still eye captured the familiar face of Congressman Hector Diaz.

Chapter 28

The slam of car doors echoed like cannon shot. Conley and a half dozen staties assembled outside Diaz's oceanfront mansion. Twin Mercedes sat in the driveway, chrome and glass gleaming in the twilight. The crisp clang of a bell buoy in the harbor tolled relentlessly.

When they were ready, Conley knocked on the front door and announced himself. No answer, a bad sign. Had he been warned? The red tape involved with arresting a sitting congressman had taken forever, and a man like Diaz had ears everywhere. And after Richard Drewicz confessed that Diaz had trafficked young girls from across the world for his pleasure, there was no telling how desperate the man would be.

Conley signaled two cops and they lugged a battering ram to the entrance. After three punches, the black cylinder shattered the eight-panel door and part of the frame. The study and living room were empty, as was the kitchen. Two empty wine glasses sat in the sink, and two soiled dishes. The rich smell of garlic and marinara hung in the air.

Music played upstairs—Vivaldi, a cacophony of violins and harps. Conley climbed the wide steps. Awards and citations lined the staircase walls—pictures of Diaz with dignitaries and fancy declarations of his service.

Tokens of goodness—smokescreens. Beware of praising the pious.

A crucifix and a painting of the Blessed Heart hung near the top. *Sacrilege.*

The images of Diaz and the children he'd seen hours before, of the monster's lustful face, were memories he could not erase. He thought of the nature of human evil, and the exponential pain it spawned, and unholstered his gun.

He thought about Lisa and her campaign manager, Bill McNulty—Diaz's opponents. Would they celebrate his arrest?

Sadness gripped him. The world was overrun with liars, perverts, and fiends. For every Channary and Sheila Thompson, for every Sage and William O'Neil, for every decent human being there seemed to be a dozen Diazes, Drewiczes, and McNultys.

And how many Paladins? Conley tightened his finger on the trigger and thought about Victor Rodriguez—an unlikely hero. Drewicz denied killing him, but admitted the fight at the sex club was about Victor's guilty conscience over the abused girls—and his vow to stop Diaz's operation.

"Congressman Diaz," Conley called when he reached the top of the stairs, surprised at the calmness of his voice. The music built to a crescendo. He pushed the bedroom door and it swung open easily. Diaz and his wife lay sprawled on the bed, eyes open and bloodshot, mouths foaming—the telltale signs of poisoning.

The easy way out. Too kind of a mercy. He holstered his gun.

Justice denied.

Chapter 29

Almost a week had passed since the death of Congressman Hector Diaz. Stefanos' team had uncovered no link to Victor's killer, and as leads diminished, they seemed destined for failure.

Conley opened the refrigerator door and soft white light spilled into the dark kitchen. He stared inside, bored and hungry. Red, yellow, and white McDonalds bags stood sentry around Lloyd's pitcher of sweet tea. Two weeks in the Nahant safe house had turned his life upside down, made him sleepy all day, restless at night, and melancholy 24/7. Faces were the problem. Haunting images. In the bedroom of the old house, a gallery of people paid visit—Lisa and her new lover, the lifeless bodies of those who had wanted Channary, Diaz and his wife, the butchered corpse of Victor Rodriguez. Even the handless body of Tommy Lopez. What the hell was happening to Ocean Park?

The refrigerator light suddenly blinked off. Moonlight painted the kitchen with a yellow glow. The oil burner in the basement clicked and went silent.

He cat-footed to the living room. Lights were off, the VCR display black. Outside, streetlight illuminated a patrol car. A porch lantern shone from the house next door.

"Power failure," Kendricks called from above. The stairs creaked as he descended.

"Just ours," Conley said. "Neighbors have power." He felt for the cell phone on his belt and fingered an empty holder.

"Hey, Conley?" Kendricks asked in a soft voice.

"Yeah?"

"You don't have my weapon, do you?"

Conley reached for his own automatic and touched the handle.

"No," he whispered. "Stay with Channary."

The lights snapped on.

Channary padded from the bedroom and stood in front of Kendricks. He placed his hands on her shoulders.

Small sounds came from the kitchen—a slight scrape across a wooden surface, pouring liquid, the chatter of a chair leg. Conley drew his gun and walked toward them.

William O'Neil and Sage sat at the table, behind Lloyd's tea pitcher and two glasses. Sage sat straight, arms folded tight, her hair in cornrows now. Her bright eyes held Conley's. O'Neil had one elbow on the table, hand squeezing a blue rubber ball.

Hardware lay on the table in front of them— Conley's cell phone, Lloyd's gun, a Nahant policeman's badge. Sage sipped from her glass.

"How'd you get by security?" Conley asked.

"Matt, my friend," O'Neil said, neck muscles flexing in time with the squeezing hand. "You have no security." The hand stopped, as if the ball had been subdued.

"But you will now."

****

O'Neil surveyed the house. An hour later, he paced

the living room and pushed the window blinds aside. Light played on the police cruiser.

"You need more police," he said to Conley. "Stagger patrol cars along the street like a W, two cops in each. They'll be hard targets."

"How'd you get in?"

O'Neil kept talking. "Station a cop in the woods nearby."

"Why'd you bring Sage?"

O'Neil pointed at the basement entrance.

"You need alarm contacts on the cellar windows. Place motion detectors in all the major pathways in the house, on every floor, battery powered. Redundant alarms with dedicated power."

Conley followed him into the backyard. A moon in a cloudless sky lit the tiny patch of grass. The ocean was almost half a mile away, but the thick smell of sea salt saturated the air. They hung on the fence and peered at the cliff below.

"Matt, the Latin Kings will come for the girl. They need to know who killed Victor Rodriguez. Or the Asian Boyz, to silence her. This wall is your protection, but a cop should still patrol the backyard every half hour or so. Vary the interval. Make it unpredictable."

"All right."

"Prepare for the unknown. Surprise is their best weapon. They'll come at you in an unlikely way."

The surf pounded. A sudden breeze rustled the vines on the fence.

"Matt, they're coming. If you didn't know that already, know it now. I'm leaving Sage with you. Tell your captain she's a doctor. She'll take care of Channary and tend to your friend's gunshot wound.

Tell Kendricks to trust her instincts."

"Why? What's going on? Where will you be?"

O'Neil's eyes were bright with moonlight when he spoke.

"Not here. It's my turn to help Ocean Park."

Chapter 30

Stefanos assigned more patrol cars to the safe house, and alarms were added. When Conley left for St. Amby's, Kendricks and Mazzarelli were testing the motion detectors. There'd be no more unexpected visitors.

Conley slowed as he drove past the church and watched hundreds of people march in a long, lazy oblong on the sidewalk. He parked at the end of the street and walked back. The smoky smell of peppers and onions grilling on a sausage vendor's pushcart sweetened the air. A woman with a paisley scarf over her hair scurried by him toward the marchers.

Captain Stefanos' prophecy had come true. News of the crying statue had turned the church into a circus. Summer Street was a carnival of cars, trucks, protestors, street vendors.

As he neared the crowd and saw familiar faces, he thought about how the myth of the crying Madonna had given renewed life to the old church. The flock were convinced magic had suddenly happened at St. Ambrose's, that something supernatural had stepped right out of the Bible and decided to pay a visit to Ocean Park.

Not that the pious parishioners had ever needed miracles to affirm their faith.

A Virgin gave birth—I believe.

Water became wine—I believe.
Christ rose from the dead—Dear God, I believe.
Or did they?

The older people stepped lively. The marchers wore heavy clothes—the dark, rumpled garments still needed in March in New England. But the crowd didn't look drab, maybe because they were wearing more than just clothes today. They were wearing *vindication* and *redemption.*

Over bovine blood.

They carried pictures of the crying statue blown up into grainy posters. One walker wore Mary on front and back like an old-fashioned sandwich board, connected with nylon straps over shoulders. Another had nailed her to a two-by-four that he carried upright, sides curling back like wings. A busty brunette wore a white T-shirt that read "Save Saint Ambrose", but mostly seniors dominated the throng, white-haired heads swaying like a wind-blown field of cotton.

He looked for Father McCarrick, but found Father Spinelli instead.

"Matt," he said. "This is insanity."

"I know."

"Talk some sense into Father McCarrick."

"I'm going to try."

"Tell him the parishioners have a new home, but they're still his flock. The pastor at St. Margaret's has offered them their old chapel."

"I'll do my best, Father."

Conley climbed the stairs to St. Amby's. The steps looked cleaner than he remembered, fresher, the grime suddenly gone. Maybe Mrs. Blodgett had scrubbed them in preparation for the news cameras, or maybe the shuffling footsteps of this new army of St. Ambrose's faithful had simply scraped them clean.

The door was open, propped by a bucket of rock salt, and candlelight flickered inside. The pews near Mary were full, people praying and talking, rosary beads clutched hard, as if they were scurrilous things that might fly away. Children wailed and fidgeted, and their parents stared intently at the pink and blue statue.

The Communion kneeler was crowded, a row of heads and backs in all shapes and sizes. Signs of the cross flew like spastic salutes, always followed by a glance at the side altar that held the miraculous piece of plaster. Hundreds of votive candles burned, an army of wax soldiers. Their light cast an eerie glow over the altar and yellowed the linen curtain on the tabernacle. They shined on the ceiling like stars, moving and pulsing.

Mrs. Blodgett had placed an aluminum folding tray near the Madonna, loaded with her homemade cookies and croissants. She was nearby, kneeling at the altar rail, in the precious space available. But prayer wasn't her mission. Her elbow pistoned as she polished the wooden rail with a wet rag. The strong pine-tree scent of furniture oil masked the mustiness of St. Ambrose's. And the altar rail shone like a mirror, as did the front pews. She'd polished the old seats to such a high gloss they looked wet.

Father McCarrick bent over a table and placed fresh candles in empty spaces. He retrieved the collection box, a square wooden job with a narrow slit wide enough for a dollar, and carried it to the sacristy. He walked with a spring in his step, and displayed uncharacteristic grace when he pirouetted, shouldered the door open, and hustled through the doorway.

Conley followed, and by the time he stepped inside, Father had unlocked the box. A pile of cash lay on the counter over the vestments cabinet. Ones, fives, and tens—wrinkled, folded, and curled, sat in a heap. Father reached into the box and drew out more.

"Matt, my boy. What brings you here on this fine, busy afternoon?"

"Quite a crowd, Father. I saw the O'Neils outside."

"I can't control who marches for salvation. Simon O'Neil hasn't stepped foot in the church, though. Probably still guilty for all that crap he pulled years ago."

"Too bad the word's out on the miracle."

"Maybe not, maybe not. Funny thing happened. Suddenly everyone wants St. Amby's to stay open." He licked the end of his thumb and counted bills into a neat stack. "Can't very well close a church when the Blessed Mother is crying about it, can they?"

"The Archdiocese, you mean?"

"Of course the Archdiocese. Those fine servants of the Lord have had a change of heart," he whispered. "The decision to close St. Ambrose has been suspended for further review. I feel bad for St. Margaret's. Collections will be a little light from now on. Our parishioners are starting to come back, Matt."

"That doesn't mean the Archdiocese will change their mind."

"Matt, my boy, you've got to understand what Church bureaucrats mean when they suspend things for review. Millenia have passed during the Catholic Church's reviews. Empires have risen and fallen. We're good for another hundred years, easy."

"It's Sunday, Father."

McCarrick looked at him and frowned. "Thanks for the reminder. I did three Masses this morning—by myself. Not an empty seat in the house for any of them. Those Boston yahoos are recalling Father Frank after seeing all this publicity, and the hard cash too, I might add. Probably put Frank to work destroying some other unlucky parish."

"Mrs. Blodgett is cooking a roast, I bet."

The priest held up a fistful of bills. "I'm not taking that bet. But since you asked, yes, just like she does every Sunday. Buys it down at the Shop-Rite on Saturday. Fresh, fat trimmed, bloody." He shrugged. "What are you, hungry? I'll have her make you a plate. There's always plenty."

"Just like she did the day the statue cried."

"Is there a reason behind this reverie or are you just trying to make my stomach rumble?"

"Father, the blood on the statue was bovine. Cow."

"Really? Interesting. God works in mysterious ways."

"But people don't."

"Meaning?"

"You used the blood from Saturday's roast to paint the statue—or Mrs. Blodgett did. I'd guess it was a team effort."

"Your imagination is vivid, Matt. I blame all those comic books you read as a youngster."

"You told me once, Father, a long time ago, that lies always mushroom. Remember?"

McCarrick packed the bills in a large canvas pouch and ran the zipper on its top. He laid the latch back down on the wooden box and hooked the padlock.

"Something happened the night Victor died, Father."

"I already told you, Matt. I know nothing about poor Victor's murder."

"I believe you, Father. But don't miss an opportunity to clear the air about the statue. Like you said, lies always mushroom—damp, ugly, and unclean."

"You missed your calling, Matt. You're a better priest than cop. Shouldn't you be out chasing poor Victor's killer?"

"I am. Pulling a thread. Seeing what unravels."

McCarrick hoisted the canvas satchel under his arm and walked to the door. "The truth is always complicated, isn't it?"

"No. The truth is usually pretty simple. People are complicated."

Father pointed to the wooden box still on the counter.

"Mind returning the money box, Matt? Give you a chance to do some good for St. Ambrose's."

Conley blocked the door. "When you're ready, Father, we'll talk."

"Of course. Always room at the table for one more sinner."

Chapter 31

That same night, Kendricks and Channary slept while Conley whispered into the phone.

"I thought you locked the church."

"I did, Matt, I did, but someone got in again. I heard moaning, a God-awful sound."

"Call the police."

"I think I just did. This is no time for games, Matt. Get over here right away."

Conley paced the dark living room. Outside, two Nahant police cars blocked the street, along with a maze of Jersey barriers. Between the added sentries and a special detachment of Massachusetts State Troopers, the place had become a very visible keep.

Kendricks stirred on the couch and pulled the blanket down from his head. He blinked. "What's up?"

"Father McCarrick's on the phone. He says someone broke into St. Ambrose's."

Kendricks sat up. "Could be important. Last person who snuck in there in the middle of the night was Rodriguez's killer."

Conley held his hand over the phone. "Ocean Park Police can check it out."

"You sure? I got a feeling this is one of those times we're gonna regret if we screw up. Could be Rodriguez's killer come back."

"All right." Conley found his jacket. "I'll go."

Kendricks punched the security code into the alarm, opened the front door, and spoke to the policeman on the steps.

"Detective Conley is leaving for a while."

"Not a problem. No one's getting past us. When will he be back, sir?"

"He'll be back when he's done, son."

"Roger that. Will SOP still be patrols around the house on the half hour, sir?"

Conley smiled. SOP. *Young buck enjoying his chance to play army.*

"That's right," Kendricks said. "That'll be SOP."

"And you open the door only for us, right, Detective Kendricks?" He nodded at the end of the street. "Or for the State boys, of course."

"Roger that, Officer."

Conley caught the car keys Kendricks threw and saluted the young cop on his way by. In the street, Conley looked back over his shoulder and hesitated. He turned, studied the house, and tried to rationalize his reluctance to leave. Lloyd and Sage were warriors, with an army at their disposal, no problem there. Maybe *he* was the problem.

Dr. Larkin evidently thought so.

Life's not all about you, Matt. Trust.

Trust.

Amen.

He continued to the car and didn't look back.

Chapter 32

"Scared, Matt?"

Father McCarrick's eyebrow lifted. He smiled, rocked from one foot to the other, and dug his hands deeper in the pockets of his cassock. A long moan came from inside the church, a quavering high note that sank into a racking cough.

"I called it in to Ocean Park Police, Father. A cruiser will be here soon."

They stood under a streetlamp, captured in a cone of light. Fast food wrappers tumbled by, trash left by the new soldiers of St. Ambrose. The smell of sausage lingered from the dark puddle of grease the pushcart vendor had dumped in the gutter. A carful of high school kids drove by, whistling and hollering.

"Sounds like a drunk," McCarrick said.

"Doesn't matter, Father. I wait for backup. That's the rule."

"Ah, yes. Bureaucracy. I understand. Nothing wrong with saying you're scared, Matt. That's why I'm out here. Of course, I don't carry a gun. Maybe I should have called Mrs. Blodgett."

"We wait, Father."

McCarrick shrugged. "Have it your way." Long minutes passed. "Did you hear that, Matt?"

Conley listened. "Sounds like more singing."

A pained wail came from inside the church. He

climbed the steps and turned at the top.

"Wait here, Father. When the police arrive, send them in."

Conley opened the door to the vestibule. The singing grew louder. A single voice didn't sound right in St. Amby's. With its deep, wide balcony and cathedral ceiling, the church was made for choirs. This cavern was built for a crowd.

Vestibule hadn't changed much. Yellowed newspapers in the corner. New holy water bowl—looked like marble, felt like plastic. Poster on the wall said St. A's was still looking for choir members. The statue of St. Ambrose looked spiffy in his new robe. Was it his imagination, or was the old boy smiling?

He cracked open the door to the church and peered inside. A garden of candles burned in front of the altar and illuminated in a way artificial lights never had. They highlighted the flecks and gold veins in the marble slab.

Simon O'Neil was strolling the center aisle, calling names to the empty pews. Names from years ago.

"Mrs. Kelly"—the old lady who played the organ. She always wore a winter coat and the kids nicknamed her The Bearded Lady because of the fur collar she kept close to her chin.

"Bill Stanton," O'Neil yelled—the old man who used to bang the gavel in the school cafeteria for Sodality Club meetings. "Gladdie Reynolds, Charlie Stewart, Arnie Bickford."

Suddenly O'Neil burst into a string of "Alleluias" and Conley decided to call William to come for him. He closed the door and dialed his phone.

The old man was singing falsetto now, an ungodly

screech that filled the church.

No answer from William. He left a message and checked the church again.

O'Neil was in the aisle before the altar now, the widest place in the church. It wasn't wide today. An eclectic collection of tables held hundreds of candles that sputtered and smoked. The stand used to sell raffle tickets was there, along with a glass-topped job from the rectory's living room, and a TV stand. The Church of St. Ambrose looked like Father McCarrick's clubhouse. Delicate tendrils drifted from the candles, clouds of white that rose toward the painted sky. Even from here, Conley's nostrils filled with the scent of candles and his throat went dry.

The old man stretched his hands toward the Madonna and moved closer. In the muted light, her cheeks shone whiter than ivory, smoother than pearls. He sang.

"Allelu-u-u-u-u-ya-a-a-a."

And moved closer.

Conley called William again. Still no answer. He started toward Simon O'Neil.

"Mr. O'Neil," he called, and the old man turned, startled, and braced himself on one of the tables that held candles. Conley held his breath as the votive candles shook, and the newer, full ones dripped wax on the wooden surface. He gripped the old man's shoulder, steadying him. O'Neil pulled away, lurching into the table edges with hip and knee, and the glasses touched, ringing like a wind chime, while O'Neil grabbed onto the altar's guardrail for support.

Matt swore sharply as candles fell. They lay broken on the floor, a field of flickering flames. Most drowned quickly in pools of molten wax. But others flared and rolled under the pews.

The lights in the church were dim, except for the spotlight on the statue of Mary. She was still as ever, arms outstretched the same way they had been for a hundred years, eyes downcast, but this time they were staring at the front pew, which was suddenly brilliant, moving, alive—and totally ablaze.

The oil-soaked benches Mrs. Blodgett had polished erupted.

Barely seconds later the next pew was engulfed in flame. Unholy smoke rose fast and high and shrouded the altar, blending with the clouds that traveled the painted ceiling. The fire crackled loudly and spewed stifling, pungent air.

O'Neil collapsed on the floor, his pale white skin almost translucent in the fire's light. A see-through hand stretched toward Conley.

Conley crooked his arm over his mouth and nose, ran to him, clasped those weak, crooked claws, and felt the heavy, hard knuckles. He dragged O'Neil toward the entrance, the old man's thin body scraping across the tile as if fighting to stay.

Fire leapt to more pews, raced to them, and hungrily ate the ancient wood.

Simon O'Neil moaned.

The red leather on the gleaming wooden altar rail melted, blackened, shrank, and disappeared. The yellow foam inside bubbled and smoked. Embers rose from the burning seats, bright orange flakes that drifted and darted, searching for more to burn.

Conley coughed, dizzy from the smoke, and looked up at the Madonna. Her blue and pink robes shimmered. The cracks in the plaster were gone. She'd been rejuvenated. Her face seemed wet. Clear tears fell from her cheeks.

It can't be.

The fire crackled. He held one arm over his mouth, lifted the old man, and shouldered the front door open. Together they collapsed onto the landing.

Simon O'Neil's moan was a croak now, a machine-like noise. The pouring smoke was laden with ash, a nasty, cloying mix that was almost liquid. Sirens blared in the distance.

And Father McCarrick lay still on the sidewalk, head turned in profile, arms limp at his sides, cassock hugging his body like a shroud.

Chapter 33

Conley found Father McCarrick's bed in the Emergency Ward. Father's face was sallow and the rest of his body looked as limp as his drooping jowls. His Johnny was loose on the shoulders and a stripe of white skin circled his neck, a pale stain where his Roman collar blocked the sunlight.

"Matt," he whispered.

"Rest, Father. Mrs. Blodgett's on her way."

"Good."

The room smelled of cleaning fluid and chemicals. A patient moaned from behind a curtain. Something plastic and hollow fell and bounced three or four times. Feet shuffled across the tile floor. Nurses whispered, their words quiet, insistent, and slow.

"Matt," he said, "if this is the end, tell Mrs. Blodgett she's a good woman. And your mother. And notify the Archdiocese."

His breathing was loud. His arm lifted again, aimless, uncertain. "Matt, what happened to St. Amby's?"

"Gone, Father."

He turned his head on the pillow, and his voice became husky. "All my efforts to save the church, wasted."

"Simon O'Neil's fine, by the way."

He shut up and nodded. Conley removed the charts

that hung from the foot of the bed on a clipboard.

McCarrick sat up and strained to see.

Conley read the top sheet and flipped a page. Graphs and tables were unintelligible, but the note on the bottom was clear. Father McCarrick had been the victim of a panic attack. He'd hyperventilated and passed out in the glow of the burning church.

"What's it say, Matt?"

Conley looked toward the empty hall and shook his head. "Maybe we should wait for the doctor to tell you."

"Damn the doctor. If it's bad news I want to hear it from you, boy, not some quack I never met."

Was this frightened, uncaring wretch the person he'd revered for so long? Was the saintly ghost behind the confessional screen really an ordinary man?

"Damn it, Matt, give me the fucking chart."

Conley held the clipboard away from McCarrick's reaching hand.

"Thrombosis, hematoma, cardiac infarction," Conley said, raising the chart like an auction paddle.

"It says that?"

"Arteriosclerosis, angina, angioplasty."

"Jesus Christ."

"Acute carcinoma."

McCarrick leaned forward, brow furrowed. "Doesn't sound good."

Conley threw the board onto a table. "It surely doesn't."

McCarrick looked toward the door, then under the curtains next to him.

"Shouldn't they be doing more for me? Shouldn't something be happening?"

"Maybe no more can be done. What happened with the statue, Father?"

"Matt, the hell with that. Call the nurse."

Conley held Father's clammy, trembling hand in both of his.

"You should have last rites, Father. Just in case."

"From you? Not a chance."

"Time is short."

McCarrick looked to the door.

"Talk to me, Father."

"Matt, I have a confession. I lied."

"I know you did."

"I was part of it. I held the ladder for Mrs. Blodgett. She painted blood on the statue with a basting brush. God forgive her. All right, I said it. Gimme penance."

"And you too, Father. Don't forget to ask God to forgive you. For Victor Rodriguez."

"Damn Victor Rodriguez! I mean it. Damn him to hell. He cost me my church."

"How so? What part did he play in your charade?"

"None. He came to the rectory that night."

"Was Channary with him?"

"Yes. He was white as a fish belly, scared senseless. Said someone was following him, and he had to get rid of the girl."

"What did he want?"

"He wanted me to take her, that's what he wanted." He wrung his hands. "What did I do to deserve this?"

"Take her? Why?"

"I didn't ask. He didn't tell. And that's the truth."

"For God's sake, Father, why didn't you help her?" Conley said through gritted teeth.

"Ever read the papers, Matt? Child found with a priest in the middle of the night? How would that have sounded?"

The man's self-centeredness was astounding. "Who else was with them?"

"No one I saw. Mrs. B. finished her business with the blood. Victor must have entered the church after we left. That damn door knob. I heard a noise and a voice, but I was scared, Matt. So I left. Then you showed up and didn't help at all, I might add."

But Conley was having none of it. He looked McCarrick in the eye. "You should have taken the girl, Father."

"I couldn't. I was just thinking of the church, Matt. Honestly. The humiliation of it."

Conley squeezed the hand hard and leaned close to McCarrick.

"It was your job. Your *vocation*. You should have taken her in."

Father's eyes closed, and when they opened their blueness had paled as if shame faded the color.

Familiar faces appeared in the doorway—St. Ambrose parishioners.

"Your flock has arrived, Father."

McCarrick glanced at the door and his eyes widened. He grasped Conley's hand and his voice pleaded. "Now what do I do, Matt?"

"I'm not the one to absolve you," Conley said. "But the people of St. Ambrose want you back. Take the job. That's your penance, Father. And forgive Simon O'Neil. After all, you have something in common. Both of you have a lot of explaining to do to Mary."

Chapter 34

Samay cried.

The man named William O'Neil placed a hand on his wet shoulder and squeezed. Samay's head was wrapped in cellophane, covered with moving beads of water that felt like silver insects travelling hungry paths. Plastic bunched around his eyes and a ragged hole split the cellophane over his mouth. From the mask, O'Neil's face appeared as distorted as a reflection in a fun house mirror.

He lifted a running hose from the bottom of the tub with his left hand and poured water in Samay's mouth-hole. The sounds of his own spits, gargles and groans bounced off the motel's bathroom tiles.

The water stopped.

"Your choice," O'Neil said. "Say all you know, shout it loud and clear. Or suffer."

Samay screamed against the plastic. His breath pumped the mask like a bellows before he spoke.

"His name is Pon. Pon is the one you're looking for."

For some reason his mouth was being filled again. He spoke faster and louder.

"Pon killed them. Victor Rodriguez. The men who came for Channary."

O'Neil's right hand returned to Samay's shoulder and massaged.

"Pon will kill me," he said at the end of his confession. He thought the comforting hand meant it was over.

More water, a third time.

Finally, when it was done and Samay's hurried breaths prevented him from speaking, O'Neil cut the tape that held him to the inverted board, helped him up, and freed his face.

"I've betrayed the devil," Samay gasped.

O'Neil squatted in front of him and held his face with a strong hand.

"No. You've helped make him a real ghost."

****

Sour breath woke Samay on Wednesday night. Vithu's hateful face loomed just inches away. His tormentor collected Samay's shirt at the collar and yanked him out of bed.

Not again. How had Vithu found out?

For three nights Vithu had punished Samay for his betrayal of Pon. For three nights Samay had endured beatings in the basement with whips and fists until his back and buttocks were raw. He didn't think he'd survive another round.

Vithu lifted him and hurled him through the bedroom door, into the hallway. Samay knew his pleas for forgiveness would draw even more punishment, but begged anyway. Maybe the right words would soften Vithu's stone heart.

"I can't. Not again. Please, Vithu. No."

Vithu dragged him to the top of the stairs and hurled him down. Every inch of his body hurt, and the tenderness became agony with each new punch and kick. The curve in the staircase saved him from tumbling far, but his body hit the plaster so hard it cracked. Samay struggled to his feet and continued ahead of his devil. He braced himself with a hand on the curved wall, and saw when he took it away he'd left handprints of blood. For the first time in his life, he decided to pray, even though he didn't know how.

Oh Great Spirit, take Vithu out of my life. Kill him, or just make him vanish. Your choice. I'll promise you anything. I beg you sincerely.

Vithu knocked him down the remaining steps and he tumbled onto the faded rug in the dark basement, into the dank, cold cellar.

Oh Great One, rip this gang's tattoo from my arm. I hate this life. I will deny my vows, even to eyewitnesses. I hate them all dearly.

The light flicked on. Pon stood in the middle of the rug, in front of the bound body of William O'Neil. His arms were tied by rope that ran over the rafters, and his legs were lashed to a metal support pole. His face was swollen and his chin rested on his chest. Bruises and welts covered his shirtless torso. Maybe tonight wasn't about fists and whips. Samay felt elated, but wary.

Vithu poised to strike Samay again, but Pon waved him off.

"My brother Samay," Pon said. "Is this the man who tormented you?"

"Yes. He's the monster."

Pon pulled a knife from a sheath on the table next to him. The knife had ornate carvings on the handle and serrations on the blade, and curved like a scimitar. He laid the flat of the blade against O'Neil's cheek.

"Here's your chance for revenge, for justice." He turned the knife and presented it to Samay.

Overhead, the floor creaked under the sound of slow footsteps. A siren wailed far away. Samay stared at the knife. Vithu paced behind them.

Kill or be killed?

"Make a choice," Pon said. He touched the taut rope. "You may show mercy. The knife can also be freedom."

Water dripped in a dark corner. The sharp sound of each drop echoed and blended into the next.

"But if I let him go, he'll kill you," Samay said. "He told me so."

Pon lifted O'Neil's head by the hair. The captive's still eyes looked brittle. "Look at him, Samay. He's defeated. The life is gone, can you see it? The resignation on his face? He doubts himself. He might welcome death. Another choice for you to consider. It's difficult, isn't it? All the choices. Don't kill him for me. I don't fear this man."

Pon's voice was hypnotic, soothing. "So what will it be, Samay? Choose wisely."

Choose wisely? What choice will save me?

Samay raised the knife to O'Neil's throat. What choice would please them? Did he have to kill to make Pon happy? And if he did, would the ghost of William O'Neil haunt him for the rest of his life?

Samay touched the rope with the knife. Pon smiled. Samay sawed with vigor and fibers popped free from the rope. Soon he was halfway through.

This is the right choice. Pon's smile says so.

Suddenly Vithu stepped forward, wrested the knife from Samay's hand, and dragged the scimitar blade across O'Neil's throat. Blood poured and darkened his pale chest and belly. Samay gasped and backed away.

Vithu balled his fist and cocked his arm. The HATE tattoo seemed to grow.

"This is strength," Vithu screamed. He reared back and punched Samay so hard he fell to the carpet. Vithu stood over him and held the knife inches from Samay's face. Blood covered the blade and guard.

"And this is justice."

****

An hour later Samay dragged the dory across ragweed and tall grass. Its bottom whispered along the growth until it clattered over small rocks imbedded in the muddy bank. It slipped into the black river silently and spun in a slow, wide arc. He secured the bow line as Pon and Vithu lifted the body of William O'Neil, wrapped with canvas and bound with rope, into the boat's flat bottom.

The moon was a sliver, stars barely visible. Vithu climbed over the transom, balancing himself with a hand on the gunwale. The sucking mud tried to keep him on land. He sat on the wood seat near the stern, inches from O'Neil's head.

Pon pushed away from shore and stepped in, feet steady in the rounded bottom. He sat in the front seat and Samay fit the oars into the half-rings. He twisted the oar handles until the paddles ran perpendicular to the water, and pulled a steady stroke that swept them into the middle of the river. The oars created tiny whirlpools and the ripples glistened in the moonlight. The wake grew into a giant fan.

The Saugus River coiled. Samay rowed around a bank and pulled hard, the metal oar locks creaking. His arms burned from the pain of Vithu's beatings, and the night air stung his raw, beaten face. His neck screamed in agony when he occasionally looked back and corrected course when he drifted too far from the middle.

Two curves later, lonely railroad tracks stretched on the berm to their right, along with dark houses shrouded in fog. Grassy banks stood on their left, jutting chins with green beards, too muddy to hold houses. Samay pulled the oars in and helped Vithu heft the body onto the gunwale. Pon lifted the cinderblock and they dropped both into the black water together. The river cratered, rippled, and smoothed.

"Food for you, fish," Vithu said.

Bubbles rose to the surface and broke in a frothy circle.

"Ocean Park is hungry since Tommy Lopez died," Vithu said. "It's our job to feed them."

The boat seesawed back and forth. Samay sat and listened. Pon answered.

"Buddha says a warrior becomes the devil he vanquishes."

"You quote Buddha?" Vithu replied. "After desecrating a church with Rodriguez's murder, after slaughtering an army in our very home?"

"You talk to fish. You should also talk to Buddha."

"I have, Pon. Our brothers are restless. They worry about money. They ask about their future, how Pon will help them. I say Pon does nothing for others, only for himself."

"Will you help them to their graves, Vithu?"

"They say I'm their savior. They say I killed Victor Rodriguez and those who came for the girl. I don't correct them. I took your sins from you, Pon. Now I'll be feared and respected like Tommy Lopez."

"Those I kill asked to die. They whispered it like the fish, Vithu, for those who chose to listen."

"Did you ask to die, Pon?" Vithu held his hand over the spot where they'd dropped the body. "What about this demon? If not for me, he would have killed you. You're a great warrior, my friend, but your work here is done. We no longer need you."

Pon stood, perfectly balanced, and drew his knife. The river hardly rippled.

"I won't leave snakes behind, Vithu."

Samay shrank to the side of the boat. Vithu stood and the boat yawed. He reached and steadied himself on the starboard edge.

Vithu and Pon faced each other. Water gently slapped the hull. Moonlight flashed on the knife suddenly in Vithu's hand.

Pon held his own dagger in front of his face like a knight presenting his sword, and whispered, "I'm listening, Vithu. When you're ready, I'm listening."

After a long time, Vithu sat down and turned his face toward the banks. Samay turned the boat and pulled a long stroke, while Pon stood still on the bow, spread-eagled and as unmoving as a figurehead.

Chapter 35

The next day marked the start of Vithu's rebellion. Samay wondered whether Vithu's newfound courage sprung from his humiliation by Pon on the river, or if somehow the spirit of William O'Neil had indeed possessed and emboldened him.

Vithu and Samay searched for Pon in the tenement and the courtyard. They found him at the end of River Street, standing under an elm, its branches frosted with fresh snow. Vithu drew a bag of white powder from his pocket.

"Your leadership has failed, Pon. Your brothers live in squalor and they cower from the Latin Kings." He squeezed the bag and held it to Pon. "This is our future."

Suddenly a police cruiser sped toward them, tires squealing, and Vithu hid the bag behind his back. Pon strolled to the curb, leaned into the car's open window, and handed a fistful of bills to the cop. The policeman hesitated, studying the three of them from behind sunglasses before handing a blue jacket to Pon, along with a cap that said NAHANT.

"Wait," Pon said and the policeman obeyed.

Pon reached behind Vithu, snatched the bag, and handed it to the cop. The cruiser sped away as Pon turned to Vithu, their faces so close they almost touched.

"This is your last chance, Vithu. Seek a life of honor, one where you don't cower and hide. Here," he said, baring his teeth and pressing the jacket and cap against Vithu's chest.

"A chance for you to show courage. It's time for Channary to come home."

****

Pon squeezed black greasepaint from a tube, and his fingertips rubbed the waxy paste on Samay's face. Pon whispered.

"Bravery sleeps in all of us, Samay. We just need to wake it."

He smeared the paint across Samay's forehead and temples, the strong fingers avoiding the cuts and bruises Vithu had inflicted. When he ran some across the upper lip, the smell of the sweet goo filled his nostrils. Soon after Pon finished, the greasepaint began to harden like a mask. Pon fit a wool cap on Samay's head.

"Wake your bravery and embrace it, my brother."

The hypnotic voice seemed to ease his pain and steel his mind. It still echoed at midnight, as Samay huddled behind a garage, arms crossed, hands clutching shoulders, and waited for Vithu. The narrow space was dark, and when he moved, an earthy smell rose from wet leaves, the damp smell of decay.

The journey across Ocean Park Harbor had been frightening. He and Vithu had travelled an ink-black sea in a twelve-foot boat, and near the edge of the harbor they'd almost been sucked to the open ocean by angry whitecaps.

Vithu's reaction? He stared straight ahead, worked the bow into waves, and ignored the frigid spray that showered them. When they finally docked, Samay felt as if he'd escaped a cyclone.

He dreaded the return trip. He dreaded Vithu.

"Samay," Vithu growled from the other side of the garage, an urgent whisper. "It's time. Come."

Samay pushed himself away from the wall and trudged through fetid leaves. Vithu led the way across a lawn, past a grill and patio chairs stacked against the back of a house. They fought through thickets and crossed two more well-tended yards. Colorful window boxes decorated the fairy tale houses, scalloped wood trim hung under the fascia, flat stones lined paths to manicured gardens.

At the back of one they came to a natural wall of stone, its jagged crags barely lit by weak moonlight. The wall rose twenty feet, until the chain link fence at its top extended the rampart another eight. They stuffed gloves in pockets and laid into the rock, found handholds, set toeholds, and started to climb. Samay was faster, his wiry frame and long arms and legs dancing like a spider's. He climbed easily, his skinny frame no burden as he walked the wall, as if Pon's deft touch and encouragement had also soothed his stiff, aching muscles.

Vithu's method was to attack the cliff. His strong hands clutched the stone, punished it, forcing his muscular body upward.

Samay stopped halfway to wait for his companion, and looked over his shoulder at the yellow ribbon of light the moon laid across the dark sea. Dangling almost twenty feet up, he felt safe here, a master of the earth, a conqueror.

They reached the top where rock gave way to steel fence. The house loomed into view, a dark square with a single lighted window. Their fingers and toes poked through the chain link triangles until they were one with the swaying wall of metal. Samay reached the top first, swung his leg silently over pipe and sharp barbs, and crept down this final obstacle. He studied the house as Vithu dropped next to him.

Vithu reached into his black police jacket, drew out the folded baseball cap with NAHANT emblazoned across it in gold letters, the clothes Pon had bought from the Ocean Park cop. He pulled the cap low, almost to his eyes.

Samay watched him don the disguise, watched Vithu fish a silver badge out of his pocket and pin it over his heart. He turned to Samay when he was done, and lifted his chin twice. Samay hid behind a bush next to the house, and watched as Vithu climbed the two-step porch and rapped on the back door.

Another knock, harder this time. Samay knew it was being answered because Vithu's face turned upward. A black man with a haunting white eye appeared, curling the shade aside. Pon had said Channary's caretaker would welcome them. How did Pon know? Was it because he knew the man? Or because he knew mankind?

Vithu saluted, pointed at the doorknob, and made a turning motion with his fingers. The caretaker held up a cell phone.

Vithu patted his pockets and shook his head no.

The caretaker pocketed the phone, walked to a box on the wall, punched buttons, and opened the door. Samay came out from the bush.

"Your back. Watch your back," the caretaker suddenly shouted to Vithu and fumbled for the gun in his holster.

Vithu drew his gun, the SIG Sauer. Its black muzzle breathed fire as the SIG barked.

The caretaker fell to the floor. Samay and Vithu hurried into the dark kitchen and stood over him, listening.

"I'm sorry, Channary," the caretaker said to no one. "So sorry." Dark blood pooled under him and spread on the tile floor.

"Lloyd?" a woman called.

The caretaker groaned and narrowed his eyes. His hand covered his chest, and blood began to bubble and stream from his mouth.

"Why did you shoot him?" Samay asked and pushed Vithu toward the wall, surprised at his own bravery.

Vithu pinned him against the wall with his forearm. The heat of the gun warmed Samay's cheeks, the smell of cordite filled his nostrils. At the front of the house there were footsteps on the porch and pounding on the door. Police were coming. Time was running out.

"Your courage has failed you again," Vithu said. "I can always count on your fear." He pointed the gun at Samay's nose.

A black woman walked in, her sleepy eyes squinting in the darkness. She looked at the caretaker, gasped, and knelt next to him.

Vithu swung the gun toward her.

She glared back at him. "You the boy they send to threaten women and children?"

Vithu smiled. He extended his arm, trigger finger white.

Suddenly Channary walked into the kitchen, half

asleep—until her eyes widened and she whispered, "Kendricks?"

She screamed when Samay lifted her over his shoulder and bolted for the door, she pounded his back and fought to get free. The woman fought him too, but Vithu smashed the SIG against the side of her head, and she sprawled on the floor next to the caretaker. Samay sprinted to the fence, Channary's cries ringing in his ears.

Chapter 36

The shrill cry of bagpipes rolled across green meadows—meadows pocked with gray headstones. The wail tumbled through skeletons formed by oak and elm branches still bare from winter, and sifted through a dense copse of pines. The music propelled an army in dark uniform, somber policemen whose black shoes whispered across the green, green grass. A copper sun in a cloudless sky played on buttons and badges as the sad-faced warriors marched down a winding blacktop lane.

Marched toward Lloyd Kendricks' bronze-colored coffin.

Conley stood at the head of the casket, still holding the gold carrying handle. Mazzarelli wheezed from the exertion of carrying the coffin. Stefanos manned the other side. His face seemed softer today. Jaw line wasn't so hard, eyes were glassy.

They stared in the general direction of Madie Kendricks and her boys—Madie in her long black dress and hat, dark lace covering her face, Kit and Leshawn in tailored black suits that looked sacrilegious on mourners so young.

The boys wore green carnations. Placing Kit's at the funeral home hadn't been easy. Leshawn tried to plug one in his younger brother's lapel, but Kit pushed him away. A tussle ensued that ended when Leshawn explained "It's for Dad."

Conley glanced under the coffin, past the green straps supporting it over the grave. Dirt crumbled from the edge of the hole, became a wisp of dust, and powdered the bottom.

Cemetery workers stood near the road, watching the curiosity of a funeral as big as a rock concert, waiting. When the minister finally spoke, it felt as if God had commenced the Apocalypse.

"Welcome the Lord into your life every day, my friends." He clutched the Bible with both hands, fingers pressed around the cover as if The Book might fly away. "Our great Lord needs to welcome you only once. And today He welcomes Lloyd, beloved husband, father, and friend."

The pallbearers stepped away from the coffin, and when they walked past Madie she caught Stefanos by the arm and locked him in place next to her. She motioned Conley to her other side. With her face hidden behind the black veil, her whispers seemed more like thoughts than spoken words.

"Thank you. Thank you for your friendship."

Stefanos' face whitened. She pulled him closer.

"Thank you for loving Lloyd like I did."

Conley closed his eyes and listened to the minister's final prayer. The hardest words stayed with him.

Eternal…everlasting…forever…

Madie gently pushed her sons forward.

Kit followed his older brother to their father. They climbed the green skirt that surrounded the grave, and Kit bent briefly to look in the deep black hole. They laid their carnations on the casket.

The silence seemed impossible. Hundreds of mourners stood motionless, and when the preacher finally walked away, it felt like a signal for the world to turn on its axis again. Sage and Sheila Thompson cried softly.

Stefanos' jaw twitched as he turned to Conley. His eyes were clear now, focused, and his thoughts needn't be spoken.

Woe to Lloyd's murderer.

Because mercy was an instrument they no longer had use for.

Chapter 37

The Massachusetts State Police laid siege to Nahant. They scoured the island for clues—for it really was an island now, cut off from the mainland with a roadblock that allowed only emergency vehicles.

Citizens complained that a police state had been created, and those who complained most were sudden targets of harsh interrogations and veiled threats. The rest of the tiny town got the message. Nahant had left the United States of America, as if the island had broken loose and floated into the North Atlantic.

Conley and Stefanos stood on a small dock with a view of Ocean Park. They'd found hemp fibers, tiny strands lodged under the base of a cleat. "Did you hear anything that night?" Stefanos said to the dock owner.

"I thought I heard a girl's voice, but the voice spoke gibberish. Maybe it was a raccoon. Lots of them around town this year."

"What did she say?" Stefanos asked.

"I told you, it was gibberish."

"Tell me the gibberish. Repeat the sound."

"I can't remember gibberish."

Conley rose from the dock. "Do you own a boat?"

"Yes."

Conley pointed to the fibers on the cleat. "You the type of guy who'd use rope on a cleat?"

"No. My lines are nylon."

Stefanos bent and looked at the strands.

"Notify the lab," he said to a patrolman.

They stood and looked toward Ocean Park. Smokestacks billowed near the Ocean Parkway, and long black clouds streamed toward downtown. Sun reflected off moving cars, sparkling like a giant necklace lain on the ground.

"She's not here," Conley said. "She's not here."

****

No place was safe from police in Ocean Park. No place. On day five of Channary's disappearance, they invaded the city. Residents complained they were more dangerous than criminals—better-manned, better-armed, and righteous. Citizen's rights were trampled along with their backyards, homes, and vehicles.

Stefanos commandeered the meeting room at Ocean Park Police headquarters and made it known everyone worked for him—local patrolmen, county sheriffs, even firemen, like it or not. The Chief of Police didn't complain. The invasion of cops had made Ocean Park the safest city in the world.

Murphy's Tap was overrun with police seeking clues. William O'Neil was nowhere to be found, and Sage could only stand by and watch as most of Teddy's customers were taken away for outstanding warrants, illegal possession of firearms or drugs, and even, in one case, failure to obey a police officer in a timely manner. Mazzarelli thought that one up.

Spring arrived, an unimportant marker. The important measure was that weeks had passed since that last night in the safe house, and they'd collected no leads to Channary's whereabouts…or to the murderer of Lloyd Kendricks.

Chapter 38

Conley rang the bell to the townhouse. He was exhausted and wired, so strung out on caffeine that the hair on his arms stood as if electrified. He rang again. Sheila Thompson opened the door, but not the Sheila Thompson he was used to seeing. This one was casual in T-shirt and jeans, and her eyes were tired and glassy. She looked like he felt.

"I saw your light on," he said.

She studied him and shook her head. "Looks like neither of us is getting any sleep these days."

She waved him inside and crossed the living room. The place was a showpiece—gleaming leather couches, oil paintings, and antiques, but her desk was a different story. Printouts and photos covered the top and the hardwood floor underneath. Empty Coke cans surrounded a laptop glowing with a collage of pictures. She sat at the desk chair, handed him a cold soda, and worked the mouse.

"Let me save these files." Her voice sounded worn and brittle. "I'm tracking chatter about Channary on Facebook and Twitter." Windows appeared and disappeared on the laptop. Smiling faces of young girls—and older ones too, mostly Asian. The older faces were more colorful, with rouge, blush, and lipstick. And less were smiling.

Her hands flew over the keyboard. "I'm also

watching Backpage and Craigslist. Reading Cambodian jokes—not funny—and a whole bunch of heartbreaking stories about other kids in trouble."

"No luck?"

"Nothing yet. Nothing but the feeling I need a shower after texting with a lot of first-class creeps. I'm out of ideas. I just wish our army was as big as the bad guys'."

"Don't worry, I have a tip," he said, pulling a chair close and sitting. "Steven Pinto. Two sources confirmed him. You have access to the Sex Offenders' Registry—SOR, right?"

"Unfortunately, yes."

"Pinto's the king of the Ocean Park perverts," he said and leaned near her to watch the screen. "He had something to do with this, I'm sure of it, but I can't find his police file. I need an address."

The Massachusetts State homepage came up. She clicked through menus, entered an ID and password, and searched.

"Here he is." A mugshot of a defiant-looking man with a high forehead and stringy hair glared. His cheeks were scarred and a wisp of a goatee dirtied his chin. She traced her finger down an extensive rap sheet printed in red and black.

"You're right, he's got quite the resume."

She turned to the next page, to the bottom block for home and work addresses. "You're not going to like this, Conley. Check out Pine Grove Cemetery. He's deceased. Died last January, complications of alcoholism. He's not your man."

He lowered his face into his open hands, exhaled, and clenched his fists. "They played me. I wasted three days on corroboration." He relaxed his hands and straightened. "Prepare yourself, Sheila." The evenness and gravity of his voice surprised him.

"What do you mean?"

"It's been too long—15 days. You know this business. They kidnapped Channary to silence her. Chances are they already have."

"Don't say that," she snapped.

The words climbed his dry throat, unstoppable. "It's better if you prepare."

"Enough."

"Face it. Every day that passes reduces her chances exponentially."

He massaged his temples with his fingertips. A buzz started inside his head, a building drone of cicadas. *I don't sleep at night. Bagpipe music keeps me awake. Little boys in black suits stand beside my bed. A widow is with them, her face hidden behind lace—and a beautiful, brown-eyed girl.*

And of course Brandon. Always Brandon.

Her voice halted their crescendo.

"You left them—Kendricks and Channary—and things went terribly wrong. You can't change that. You had to make a decision."

"The wrong one."

"Forget it. I know what Channary would do."

"What?"

"Pray."

The room became eerily quiet. The digital clock on the mantel blinked and changed to midnight.

"Right," he said and rolled his eyes.

She folded her arms. The photo of Steven Pinto—the late Steven Pinto—flickered behind her.

"Channary believed in prayer," she said.

Wind rattled the windows. A dog barked in the next townhouse and stopped abruptly. He stared at her long and hard before setting the can on the desktop. He laughed.

"Channary's just a child."

"A very precocious child. She was teaching us a lesson, Conley."

"Wonderful. I haven't got time for this." He stood and stretched. A calmness came over him. The caffeine had worn off, leaving nothing but the sting of acid indigestion—and a millstone of regret. "I'm sorry. I'm just frustrated. I'm so very sorry."

She clicked off the computer, sat back in her chair, and took a long drink. She waited a full minute before answering.

"Apology accepted, on one condition."

He spread his arms and opened his hands.

She leaned forward and her breath smelled like sweet apples. Her face, her porcelain face, so fresh and serious, so different from the hard, made-up face at the Paladin, was all he could see.

"Don't give up."

The words hung in the air. Her voice was gristle and sandpaper, filled with resolve.

"Don't get frozen, Conley. Look forward, not back. To hell with the past. Don't sleep, don't get frustrated, and whatever you do, don't stop. Don't stop until you find Channary."

****

Samay climbed the steps to Ocean Park Police Headquarters on the first Monday in April. Cops brushed by, hurrying in and out. He averted his eyes and cursed as he prepared to carry out another dangerous task from Pon.

When would they end?

The policeman Conley was waging his own personal war on River Street. He wouldn't find Channary there, but what else would he discover? Would one of the gang crack? Would they make a mistake and give him the answer he sought? Conley followed the gang constantly, randomly, like a lamprey on fish. He sat in his car in the courtyard at night, behind tinted windows, and his invisibility was more disturbing than his spectacle. There seemed to be an army of *him*—watching, following, asking questions. Worst of all, he couldn't be bought or bullied like the other Ocean Park cops.

Madness.

Sooner or later, someone would talk because Conley's face said he would die before giving up. When Pon gave Samay his latest mission—in the dark of night—for the first time his leader seemed to lack composure.

Samay stopped at the front desk. Glass protected a cop with heavy gray glasses who worked a computer. Behind him stood a bank of desks, mostly empty, and a solid wall of metal file cabinets. A man with hair as black as shoe polish sat at one of the cluttered desks, writing on a yellow pad, phone cradled to his ear.

Finally, the busy computer cop turned, dipped his head, and peered at Samay.

"What can I do for you?" the cop asked through silver vents in the metal circle in the glass.

"I want to talk about the girl named Channary."

The cop adjusted his glasses. He whistled to the

man on the phone and turned back to face Samay.

"You and half the city. Detective Mazzarelli will take your statement. That's about all he does these days."

Chapter 39

The Asian boy named Samay led Conley and four speeding police cruisers to a crowded neighborhood that bordered the Boston and Maine railroad tracks. Tenements loomed on both sides of a narrow street, their shadows darkening the cars that hurtled past. Gray pulleys on third-floor window sills held dingy clotheslines that stretched high overhead, sagging with the weight of sheets and blankets that swung and snapped. Shafts of light peeked from small spaces between close buildings and flashed on the speeding convoy like a strobe.

They braked in front of the three-family at the street's dead end. Conley and Thompson stepped out of the lead car. He looked back. Cruisers blocked the exit to the main street. Neighbors gathered on balconies and porches, pointing. A cool staleness blanketed the dark courtyard, covering it like wet gossamer.

Something was strange about this house. Different. Conley had felt it as soon as they turned the corner and saw the pale blue apartment building blend into the crystalline sky above it. This place had something to tell.

Something we need to know.

Car doors opened and slammed in the quiet courtyard. Stefanos took a step forward and surveyed the house, the peeling paint on asbestos shingles, the dirty windows, the rickety porch. An army of trash barrels stood on a patch of soil. Broken lattice sat near the dark opening that led under the porch.

Mazzarelli climbed the steps and knocked on the plain wood door, dull knocks echoing in the still morning.

Samay stood in back, cops flanking him.

Stefanos turned to the other houses as they waited, and considered every window, every tilting porch.

Mazzarelli knocked again, slower, harder, longer.

An old man with skin the color of milk chocolate opened the door. Wisps of salt-and-pepper hair plastered his scalp. He shuffled outside, sandals scraping the porch. Mazzarelli showed his badge and Channary's picture as he spoke.

The man listened, nodded hard, and leaned toward the gathered crowd.

"No girl here," he called. "No girl." He held his pudgy hand up in a quick salute, pointed fingers down, and waved his backhand at them in a shooing motion. "Sorry. Good-bye."

Mazzarelli spoke. "This is Mr. Desh, Captain. He owns the building. Says the girl's not here."

"No shit, Mazzarelli," one of the local cops muttered.

"Ask him if we can take a look," Conley said.

Desh headed back to the house. Mazzarelli blocked his way and started talking again, selling the idea with lively, coaxing hands that carved the air between them. Desh lifted his chin to avoid the flying mitts and adamantly refused. Mazzarelli used a lull in the bickering to give an update.

"He wants a search warrant. Says he knows his

rights."

Suddenly Samay broke away, strode past the trash barrels, and stood at the head of the narrow alley next to the house. He lifted his arm and pointed to a rusted metal bulkhead attached to the house's foundation like an ugly tumor.

Stefanos walked to the hatch.

Desh ran to them, knees high, sandals flapping. He crossed his arms and stood in front of the bulkhead like a sentry.

"No," Desh said insistently, head turning back and forth so hard his jowls shook. "You have no rights here," he said, pounding his chest with the side of a fist. "I'm not scared of Cups."

Cups.

"You go away now. Right now."

Sheila put her hand on Conley's shoulder. Stefanos reached in his jacket and drew his automatic. Desh's eyes widened and his pleas jumped several octaves. Stefanos held the gun upright and locked eyes with the harried landlord before he spoke.

"Step out of the way, Mr. Desh."

****

One side of the bulkhead swung upward with a long, aching creak, and locked on its hinges with a twang. Three wooden steps led down—rough, unfinished planks without risers—to a green door. Conley went first, descended the stairs, and pressed the thumb latch on top of the curled handle. He pushed his knee into the door and it protested, swollen wood holding tight at header and jamb. A kick worked. The door scraped open with a loud crack.

The dank cellar was filled with junk. Old, hard

suitcases sat in columns on his right, handles and straps hanging from them as if tired from traveling. A gritty path was on the left, a way through the mountains of debris. Light shone through narrow windows milky with grime.

Stefanos and Mazzarelli followed. Mr. Desh started up again outside, beseeching the unanswering cops, his muted, hurried voice drifting through the open bulkhead.

"I tell you no girl, no girl, no girl," he chanted.

Conley shut him out as they zagged left along the path, past an old steamer trunk with a gouge on the top that showed the brown board it was made of. A discarded, rust-colored washing machine sat to the left, top lid missing, knobs gone too, wires snaking from the naked control panel.

Something round was next, big as a barrel—a sheet metal canister with holes like a giant colander.

They passed a pegboard that held a collection of awls and chisels, old, gray, and dull. The wooden handles were wrapped with frayed electrical tape. The workbench under the board had a dark, round stain in the middle of its battered countertop. Tools hung from nails in the rafters. Conley pushed aside a row of hacksaws and the blades clanged, singing like dull chimes.

They turned a corner, past leaning towers of cardboard boxes lined with white, crusty calcium.

A tattered bamboo screen stood at the end of the aisle, dim light filtering through its tiny slats. A wisp of steam escaped, climbed over the top of the screen like a living thing, and tumbled toward them. Metal clinked, a faint sound.

Stefanos and Mazzarelli stood on either side of Conley as he clutched the screen's edge—and pulled it aside.

Channary sat on blankets on the floor, a picture book on her lap, a reading light over her shoulder. One of the Aunties squatted next to her on her haunches, a kettle boiling and clattering on a hot plate in front of her.

Channary looked up from the book and smiled.

Conley did something he hadn't done in a long time, indulged in a luxury he didn't think he was capable of anymore.

He smiled back.

Chapter 40

Conley watched from a crowded sidewalk still wet from the first rainstorm of April. Mazzarelli was waiting to cross Cambridge Street, the four-lane racetrack that fed Boston's busy downtown. The tips of Mazzarelli's Oxfords aligned perfectly with the edge of the curb. Pedestrians gathered beside him.

One Central Plaza loomed above, a long, sweeping, macaroni elbow of a building whose curved design allowed a panoramic view of City Hall and Government Center. Perfect place for Boston's FBI Headquarters.

The pedestrian signal flashed WALK in bright white letters and Mazzarelli meandered onto the street with the crowd, parading in front of idling cars and trucks. He passed skyscrapers, swinging his leather briefcase in the crisp morning, nearing the wide steps to City Hall Plaza. Conley stepped out from behind a concrete wall next to the staircase and fell into lockstep.

The briefcase stopped swinging

"Conley, what are you doing here?"

"Spying on you, Mazzarelli."

Mazzarelli looked back over his shoulder at FBI Headquarters, head pecking like a pigeon's as he counted up six floors and scanned the long row of curved windows.

"They'll see us. We're out of this now. The feds have taken over the Diaz and Rodriguez investigations.

The EFF-BEE-EYE, Conley."

"It's Friday. You've been up there all week. What did you learn from them?"

"Nothing," he said, banking left between parked cars and dashing across the street ahead of a swarm of traffic. Conley tried to follow, but speeding cars blocked him. The swoosh of traffic blew his hair back, ruffled his clothes, and watered his eyes with high-octane exhaust.

Mazzarelli hopped onto the sidewalk across the street and hurried past restaurants and souvenir shops. Quincy Market was just ahead.

Sheila Thompson stepped beside him and matched his lope.

"Mazzarelli, how's Channary?"

Mazzarelli almost stumbled, and looked back at the building again.

"You're not supposed to be doing this," he hissed.

"Neither are the feds," Conley said, catching up. "Tell me, Mazzarelli. What are they up to?"

Mazzarelli started off again, but they were faster, cutting him off, working together like tugboats slowing a ship. Conley and Thompson got in front of him and blocked his way. Two faces spoke one question after another like a very persistent Siamese twin.

"What's their next step, Maz?"

"Who are they questioning?"

"Is Channary okay?"

"Did they arrest Desh?"

"Listen," Mazzarelli said. "A congressman's been accused of child trafficking and now he's dead. The FBI has jurisdiction. They impounded my case files."

"And they couldn't care less about who murdered

Lloyd," Conley said.

Thompson leaned into Mazzarelli's space.

"So you're telling us you just spent three hours with the FBI and you know nothing. Absolutely nothing at all."

A horn blared behind them on Clarendon Street. She held her place, warm breath steaming like a locomotive, bright brown eyes locked on his.

Mazzarelli adjusted his glasses and sunlight glinted.

"I wouldn't say nothing."

****

That night at Morgan's Tap, Conley tapped his fingers on William O'Neil's desk. Mazzarelli was on the other side sorting a stack of paper. Sage paced behind them, listening.

"The FBI finished interrogations," Mazzarelli said. "They capture the data on these forms—FD 302s. They're not transcripts. They're summaries."

"How'd you get them?" Stefanos asked.

"The FBI Information Management Assistant left them in the copy room."

"You made illegal copies of a federal investigation?"

Mazzarelli sat straight and adjusted his tie.

"I did."

Stefanos nodded, smiled, and turned to Thompson and Conley. "Read through these. Look for inconsistencies. Look for Lloyd's killer."

Mazzarelli removed the top one and handed it to Thompson. The thickest one went to Stefanos, the third to Conley.

Conley and Thompson sank into the leather couch.

Stefanos chose the hard chair next to the desk.

The room was quiet, but sounds from the bar seeped through the door. Glasses and bottles clacked. Voices chattered, chairs and tables clattered across the wood floor. Stale, pungent cigarette smoke drifted inside like a curious mist.

Conley read.

Raul Desh.

The landlord from Winston Place told his life story with emphasis on the trials and tribulations of owning a six-family in a city of immigrants, poverty, and crime. Leaky pipes, finicky furnaces, and holey roofs. Vandals, bums, and neighborhood punks haunted his days and sleepless nights. India didn't seem so bad after a few years toiling in Ocean Park. If he wanted to make a few extra bucks for an illegal apartment in his basement, where was the harm?

Where was the harm?

Conley read the last page and looked up. Thompson had finished her file. They waited like kids after an exam, and when Stefanos finally lifted his head, Mazzarelli said, "Switch."

Thompson handed him…

Channary.

He imagined her smiling brightly, sitting at a big table, and answering questions from serious guys in suits. Plain, simple, and honest, that was Channary. They asked her questions and she told them answers, answers with a little extra, innocent observations and feelings from someone who, despite what she had been through, still thought the world was a good place.

She remembered a sleepy journey with strangers, a boat trip in the middle of the night. The air was cold, and waves wet her clothes and made her freeze. Then a quick car ride to her basement apartment, and weeks spent with Aunt Maly and the funny Mister Desh. Wind blew through dirty cellar windows. The noisy furnace smelled like a wet, smoky fire.

The report ended with her questions to the FBI—"Where's Conley? Is Kendricks all right?"

Conley sat back and fought tears.

Sage left, but soon came back with Teddy, who carried a tray of white mugs of black coffee. He wore a pained smile; a grimace that looked like it might break his face. He kept his head down, laid the oval tray on the edge of the desk, and backed out of the office like a manservant.

They took cups and traded stacks.

Last folder...

Samay.

High school dropout. Father unknown, mother living in Newport Beach. The Aunties took care of him too. Talented soccer player at Ocean Park High who might have won a ticket to higher education had it not been for a truancy record as fat as a phone book. Samay was between jobs, mostly crewing on lobster boats, day work that was hard, low-paying, and sporadic.

Conley read the meager background and flipped to an appendix, Samay's statement to Mazzarelli that led to Raul Desh's basement.

He finished the short report and re-read it, then dropped the folder on the floor and took Channary's file from Thompson. He ruffled through the pages and pulled one out of the pile.

The others stopped reading, watched, and waited. Conley spoke.

"Samay says he spotted Channary in a 7-11 in McDonough Square and followed her to Desh's house."

He held the two sheets in the air.

"Channary said she never left the basement."

Glass tinkled in the bar. Voices murmured.

"So who's telling the truth?" Mazzarelli said.

"Channary, that's who," Conley said, making eye contact with each of them, like a prosecutor coaxing a jury. "Why would she lie?"

****

When they were done, Mazzarelli gathered the folders, straightened their contents, and fit them carefully into his briefcase. Thompson and Stefanos filed out of the office behind him. Sage placed her palm on Conley's chest and told him to wait.

She walked behind the desk and opened the bottom drawer. It slid easily, scraping along the metal track, echoing hollowness. She did the same with the others, one by one, pulled them back and pushed them forward, her eyes on his. Conley glanced past her and noticed William's framed pictures were missing and the desktop was clear.

"William's gone," she said.

"Where?"

She closed the last drawer and turned away. Tears welled. "I don't know."

Conley took her hand away from the pull and wrapped his arms around her.

"I'll find him, I promise."

She pushed him away.

"This obsession of yours took him from me," she said. "It became his curse too. You brought this into our lives. I wish he'd left you bleeding on the floor."

"Sage, I'll find William. In the meantime, I can't find Lloyd's killer without you. I need help."

She placed her palms on her cheeks, dried her tears, and blew a long breath.

"At least he taught you that," she said.

Chapter 41

On Sunday night, Conley watched Samay through a coffee shop window. Samay sat on a stool at the counter, studying a young waitress as if she were prey. She balanced a tray on her delicate left hand and plucked donuts from the silver platter with her right. She placed the pastries in neat rows on slanted, well-lit shelves, careful to join them with others of their own kind. The upper part of her tanned arm slid in and out of her short sleeve like a gold piston. The white uniform caressed slender hips, stretched across a slim back and under a spill of hair so light their colors almost matched.

Samay's legs encircled the metal shaft under him—there seemed to be more joints than just ankle and knee. Elbows rested on the countertop with wrists bent and hands pecking at a cruller on the dish in front of him. He dissected the food slowly and popped torn pieces into his mouth. Steam rose from the paper cup in front of him, curled, and dissipated.

He said something to her, cheeks full, mouth still chewing. She ignored him. He spoke again, several times, until she finally turned, unsmiling, and spoke back.

He laughed and spun on the stool.

The girl walked into the back room, show over. Samay unwrapped his legs and drained his cup before he left.

Conley followed.

****

Minutes later, Samay took a quick look over his shoulder, saw darkness, and decided to light up. He brought a fat joint out of his pocket, ends twisted like taffy. He admired its heft and the tightness of the roll, and ran his tongue along the gummed seam. He lit up.

Lori liked him, he was sure. Girls always played a part, acting angry and irritated. He ran his tongue again, this time across his upper lip. He tasted sugar from the donut she'd given him, the one she'd touched.

I wonder if Lori tastes as sweet?

Another pull on the joint. He inhaled and felt his lungs warm. The familiar hum began in his head. A new world was coming.

The dark sidewalk stretched in front of him, a beautiful lane with lush hedges and trees that formed a green canopy under a hazy half moon. Music drifted from a house, from windows with rippling curtains and mysterious silhouettes behind them. He smiled and held the joint sideways, appreciating the beauty of the glowing tip.

Vithu's ganja—Good stuff.

A car's engine surged from behind, growling like an animal. Suddenly a dark metal behemoth jumped the curb, tires carving tracks in the thin strip of sidewalk grass.

Samay stared, frightened, as the car stopped in front of him. Dark tinted windows hid the inside, and he wondered if a driver was behind the wheel or if the angry vehicle was acting on its own. A click sounded, the wide trunk yawned, and the lid quivered.

A tiny bulb reflected on something inside. He approached, more curious than afraid. Was this another of Vithu's games? A shovel lay on the floor, rocking back and forth. The wood handle was pocked with light-colored scars, the pointed gray blade mottled with dirt.

Strong hands clasped his arms from behind, powerful fingers clamped his triceps. Samay punched and kicked, and stiffened his body as he was forcefully fed into the trunk. The lid slammed shut and the car growled again and accelerated. A breath of greasy exhaust seeped into the closed space.

He felt overhead and ran his hand across the roof of his prison. The car banked and he was pressed against cold metal. Another turn and he slid, shoulder biting into the rear quarter on the other side.

Stop. Accelerate. The darkness got darker. Was the trunk really closing in on him? He reached out, tentatively, and touched the lid to determine if it was closer than before.

The car slid to a stop on rough surface and the trunk lid opened again, quiet and slow. Hands grabbed at his clothes, found belt and collar, and dragged him out. He fell on hard ground.

Another kind of smoke filled his lungs. Light shone from a high, crackling fire. Conley and Stefanos—the cops who had found Channary—stood between him and a blazing campfire. They wore heavy clothes—boots, jeans, pullover tops whose long sleeves ended in black gloves, and their faces were marbled red from the flames. Conley reached into the trunk and retrieved the shovel. It passed over Samay slowly, as if levitating.

Conley turned and marched away, shovel resting

on his shoulder like a rifle.

Samay stood and sprinted around the perimeter, but couldn't find the road they'd come from, or even a path in the black woods. Trees surrounded the clearing, undulating shapes that turned sea green as light flickered on leaves. A howl came from nearby, an anguished sob that cut through the crackling fire. A black woman stood next to a tree, arms held above her head by a rope slung over a branch.

He recognized her dark, tight hair and handsome face. She'd been at the house in Nahant the night they took Channary. So Vithu hadn't killed her after all. But why was she here?

Samay stood unsteadily. A beat began behind him, a metallic sound.

Chock. Chock.

He turned. Conley was thrusting the shovel into the ground on the other side of the fire. Stefanos stood behind, next to smoke ghosts rising from the blaze.

Samay shuffled to the writhing girl, his legs still aching from the ride. He slowed as he neared. She saw him and stopped.

"Help me," she pleaded.

Chock. Chock. Chock.

The fire's light made a long shadow behind her, a giant marionette, all legs and arms, a tall, black cobweb against the thick forest. Samay watched his own slow shadow join hers as he approached—until a third shadow grew. Stefanos. Samay turned to him.

"Why have you done this?"

Stefanos stepped past him toward the girl. She lifted herself on the rope like a gymnast, muscles straining before her arms went limp and she fell back.

He swung a backhand, high and hard, that knocked her face to the side. Stefanos put his face in front of hers and spoke evenly.

"Who killed Lloyd Kendricks?"

Samay stepped back.

Vithu. This was about Vithu.

Her head lolled and she cried.

"I don't know. You have to believe me. I don't know."

And she doesn't.

Slap. "You were part of it. Last chance."

Chock. Chock. Chock.

Stefanos repeated the question over and over, his voice smooth and deep.

"Who killed Lloyd Kendricks? Who killed Lloyd Kendricks? Who killed Lloyd Kendricks?"

Did he say it three times—or three hundred? The question became a string of sounds, words that made no sense. Samay stumbled away, the gibberish ringing in his head. He crossed the clearing, closer to the *chocks.* Conley was working, chest-deep, in a long, narrow hole. Sweat poured from the young cop's brow and his face was dark crimson now. Samay slowed and stepped back when he realized the devil was toiling in a grave.

A shot rang from behind. Samay turned, saw the black girl go limp, arms drawing the ropes taut, legs bending and swaying. Stefanos cut her ropes and her lifeless body fell to the ground. Samay collapsed to his knees, placed one palm in the loose dirt, and pointed back to the still girl.

"Why have you done this?"

Conley turned and looked back at the dead girl with mild interest.

"Because she might have known."

Might have known?

Stefanos was behind him again. The man moved magically around this hellish knoll. He just kept appearing, still as stone. He held the gun loose by his side, and when Samay looked at it, the automatic rose to greet him.

He watched the gun lift, one with the glove and dark sleeve, and stared at the hole in its end, wondering if he'd be able to see the bullet when it left the barrel.

Stefanos said, "Who killed Lloyd Kendricks?"

Samay laughed.

Was this their plan? Kidnap every person who breathed the same air as the murdered cop—then question—then kill?

"Who killed Lloyd Kendricks?"

Did they think he'd betray the gang? Never again. They wouldn't just kill him for betrayal, they'd make Samay an example for new Asian Boyz. Hell only knew what they had in store—boil him alive maybe, skin him, crucify him. Those were the torments Vithu liked to talk about now that Pon was gone—back to Cambodia, some said.

Samay would rather the bullet. At least death would be quick.

A third time.

"Who killed Lloyd Kendricks?"

"I don't know."

Conley was neck deep now, but he managed to reach out and snare Samay's ankle.

"Don't waste the bullet," Conley said.

Stefanos nodded and lowered the gun.

Conley pulled Samay's leg toward the hole. He

bent, hands bracing the ground, and tried to kick free. Stefanos clamped his biceps with steel fingers and helped him toward the grave. One leg cleared the edge and Conley pulled it hard toward the bottom. Stefanos denied any purchase, lifting Samay's hand every time he clawed at ground.

Both legs were in the hole now. Conley swept Samay's legs out from under him and pushed his shoulders into the bottom. Samay tried to rise, but a foot pinned the small of his back.

A clump of soil punched him between the shoulder blades and rained silently over his torso. Another, pounding his legs this time. The third fell on his head and when it disintegrated, the particles of dirt felt like crawling insects invading eyes and ears.

He shut his mouth tight, but then his nose breathed the musty soil. He moved his face to the side, searching for a pocket of clean air.

Soil came faster. The heavy foot anchored him, pressing him into the bottom of the grave.

"Mercy," he screamed through a spray, and was answered with another shovelful.

The earth seemed to be crawling over him quicker, a swarm of cold mites. He spat mud and yelled, "Vithu. Vithu killed your friend. Have mercy!"

Another shovelful came, and for a frozen second he thought he heard the scrape of the blade again. He waited. And waited.

A minute or an hour?

Samay stirred and found he could turn. He raised his head and shook it clean. His legs moved as he twisted and rolled like a worm. He stood and climbed from the hole.

The car was gone, and the girl. The fire was dying. The shovel lay on the edge of the hole.

He sank back on his knees.

Vithu—the new, powerful Vithu—would wreak revenge on him. He'd sworn allegiance, vowed not to snitch, and was aware of the consequences. What form would his vengeance take? Samay shuddered, not from the cold, or from the wind that whistled through the sleeping trees. He hugged himself, rubbed arms pocked with goose bumps, and wondered what kind of nightmare he'd bargained for.

Chapter 42

Conley and Stefanos laced their fingers through the chain links of the fence around North Shore Salvage on Monday night and peered through the diamonds formed by the silver steel. River Street lay on the other side. A dark train of black SUVs with tinted windows sat next to the curb.

A woman in a blue jacket left a van and entered the middle building. FBI was stenciled on the back of her coat in mustard-colored letters. CRIMES AGAINST CHILDREN was written underneath. Conley's fingers tightened against the steel.

They waited. Cars came and went, and by the time night fell only one was left.

They walked wide to avoid it, traipsing through the overgrown riverbank and backyards to hide from the street. Stefanos entered the last tenement through an unlocked door, Conley right behind. After all the horror that had happened here, the Cambodians' trust in mankind hadn't been shaken.

Sounds and smells—the racket of clattering pans, the aroma of cooking oil, the hiss of food frying.

Second floor was the target. That's where Vithu lived. They climbed silently, drew their guns, and entered the apartment. A sandwich sat on a plate on the kitchen counter, untouched. Stefanos and Conley continued through a doorway.

An open room had been turned into separate cells by hanging sheets. Aluminum tracks in the ceiling supported straightened planes of fabric, most in bright colors, many of them hand painted.

A lion peered from one, mouth open, lips baring teeth that looked as big as a saber tooth's. Its orange and black mane stretched across the width of the curtain.

Buddha was painted on another, a bright-eyed, happy Buddha. The world spun behind it, a globe that exaggerated the size of the peninsulas of Southeast Asia. Children and old women worshipped their god from both sides with uplifted faces and praying hands.

Conley moved the sheets. The cubicles held empty beds and simple furniture.

A skin tag told them Vithu had imagined a green mountain paradise, and painted his sheet with the vision. They passed through a doorway into another room of curtains, to a third cubicle. A green mountain stood in front of them, a steep, lush rise thrust upward into a brilliant blue sky. Giant palm trees were painted on both sides of the mountain, disproportionate giants that held too-round coconuts hanging under graceful fronds. A waterfall cascaded down the mountain face.

Conley braced himself as Stefanos threw the curtain aside.

The curtain to Paradise.

The room was empty. A wood floor, so clean and shiny it looked wet, made it hard to believe anyone had ever lived there.

Movement behind. They turned.

A boy with sleepy eyes stood in front of them. He popped a last bit of sandwich into his mouth, wiped his hands on his chest, and spoke a garbled message.

"Sorry, my friends," he said. "Vithu doesn't live here anymore."

****

In the room above Vithu's, Channary lifted the suitcase onto her bed and ran a hand over the top. It was a gift from Sheila—purple, her favorite color. Slowly, she folded her clothes and packed them, then sorted her books. She couldn't take them all. Some she selected because she loved the cover. Others she took for the words inside and the happiness they'd given her. She placed the leftovers on her absent roommates' beds.

Even with her pared-down book collection, the suitcase was heavy, too heavy to lift. She pulled the bag off the bed and onto the floor with a thud.

Two quick knocks startled her. The door swung open and the Aunties came in, greeting her with smiling faces. They wore fancy clothes today, with prints and embroidery. Funny to see their necks bare, without kramas to wipe their faces and hold back their hair.

One by one they gave her gifts—ceramics, carvings, hand-crafted jewelry. Each of them hugged her and she clung to the folds in their clothes, soft and warm. Maly—the first one she'd met who had taken her hand so long ago, the one who'd cared for her in Mr. Desh's basement—hugged the longest. Channary would miss her the most.

Time to leave. Maly lifted Channary's suitcase easily and clasped Channary's hand with her strong one, and together they left the bedroom in a line, like a sacred procession. Sheila arrived and joined Conley and Stefanos in the darkening courtyard. The plastic wheels on the purple suitcase crackled on the concrete. A woman in a blue FBI jacket held open the door to a black car. Dust motes danced in its headlights.

Channary turned and hugged Sheila. The sketchbook Channary carried under her arm kept falling, so she made a quick decision. With a heartfelt smile, she stepped back and presented it to Sheila. Sheila's smile then wobbled as she offered her thanks, tears brimming in her eyes. Channary hugged Stefanos and Conley next, then squeezed their hands in between both of hers and thanked them for their kindness to her in English,

She climbed into the car. The door closed behind her and the engine started. She looked back and saw many shining faces in the darkness, like a sky with sparkling stars.

She was going home at last, to friends, her mother, her brother. Strange how the anticipation of happiness could also bring tears.

Chapter 43

Vithu's dream had come true—for him. Samay watched Vithu's Lexus approach in the darkening twilight, chrome and black metal gleaming. Vithu lived away from the tenements now, and his drug business paid for a luxury apartment and a fleet of new cars. The gang had become his personal servants, muling coke and heroin. And Pon?

Pon was nowhere to be found, and rumor was Vithu had put an end to him so he could become the new leader of the Asian Boyz. Vithu himself hinted that Pon shared the same grave as William O'Neil.

The Lexus' headlights lit the road between them, and Samay felt like the blinding beam blazed in inquisition whenever he stood before it. Vithu stepped onto the road, retrieved a duffle bag from the trunk, and slowly came forward. The diamonds in his gold pinky rings glittered, and the thick chain on his neck shifted with each step.

"Samay," he said, smiling. "Bring this to your brothers, Samay. Tell them to work through the night—cut the product and deliver it. And tell them to be grateful, Vithu's the one looking out for them now."

Samay bowed his head and slung the heavy bag over his shoulder. Vithu had won; to fight against him was pointless because he was everywhere, all-seeing, all-knowing. The Asian Boyz were slaves to Vithu now, until the day they were caught and imprisoned—or killed.

He watched Vithu head back to his car and turn the ignition key. The motor turned but did not catch. Odd—the lights were bright and the starter whirred insistently.

Samay adjusted the strap that bit into his neck and turned to the courtyard, trudging through cloying mud, past a high stand of still weeds, The growth rustled behind him, the straining straps relaxed, and the bag fell away.

Samay turned. Pon held the bag with one hand and sliced a knife through its side. White powder spilled out and drifted across the weeds like a cloud.

"Go home, Samay," Pon said and headed toward the car. "Tell the others to sleep. Tell them peace has come."

****

A week after Channary left, Conley and Stefanos answered a call to the bank of the Saugus River. Spring rain had thickened ragweed and cattails. Dark ruby eyes stared through the brush. A pink pair joined them. The rats blinked, almost in sequence, and waited.

Flies and maggots didn't. They crawled over Vithu's dead flesh and made it seem a living thing.

Conley stood over the corpse as cops strung crime scene tape around them. The body lay on its back, face staring at the sky, arms spread, legs straight, as if crucified on the cloying gray mud. The face was intact. The hole in his chest must have been an easier meal.

The right hand held a gun—*Lloyd's undeserved fate*—a new SIG Sauer gleaming with moisture. The left held a knife—just as wet, reflecting a single point of light, a kiss from the setting sun.

A gift.

From who? Did it matter? After so much bad luck and heartache, why question an unexpected bit of good fortune for Ocean Park?

He studied the corpse for a long time. A warm breeze teased the tall grass and rippled the river.

Conley signaled a patrolman and dispatched him to notify the Aunties. One of them needed to identify the body, but not here, not now. He left Vithu and combed the area. Rusted junk, the same color as the earth, seemed to be melting and bleeding into the ground. Plastic grocery bags, wrinkled and bunched, caught on high weeds, a stiff breeze filling them like wind socks.

Conley worked his way to the water, leaving wooden stakes as markers for the crime scene techs. He plunged a stick into the soil near a footprint that looked fresh, also marked a piece of newspaper that hadn't yellowed yet. A campfire had burned in a clearing. Charred, ribbed bits of wood were all that remained.

A brown drop line ran a serpentine course across the sand. Rowboats lay tilted on the beach, dull gray oarlocks thrust upward from their gunwales.

He spun an oarlock and remembered the sound and feel of the straining oar when he and Lloyd rowed together so long ago. The delicious pull that brought movement, the rush of sliding across the glassy harbor, the small sounds of the oar blade in the still harbor, stirring, swirling, dripping, waking the water. These were working boats too, seats worn from tackle boxes, sun, rain, writhing eels, struggling fish. Knife marks decorated the wood, scars from honest work.

Dark puddles sat in their holds. A plastic milk jug, handle intact, its top cut open to make a bailer, floated on the puddle, tacking back and forth under a pleasant gust, passing over a treasure glittering in the dark water.

Conley knelt and reached toward the sparkle. The water was greasy and cold, thick and heavy. He felt a small chain with smooth plates attached, and lifted it out of the water. Sage's words regarding the relationship between her parents, and between herself and William, came to him.

See without sight.

He closed his fist, felt the small, freezing beads numb his fingers, and squeezed the plates so hard the edges dug into his palm. He ran fingertips over engraved letters.

Speak without words.

He sank back in the fetid mud, opened his hand, and let the last rays of a brilliant sunset shine on the dog tags.

William O'Neil's name was cut into the hard metal in stark letters—deep, straight, and bold.

Chapter 44

Divers found William's body in the deepest part of the Saugus River the next day. Had it been elsewhere, low tide would have revealed it before crabs and bottom feeders had taken their toll. There'd be no long-box and silk pillow viewing for what was left of William.

Conley and Sage brought the news to William's parents. Simon was inconsolable, but Sage did her best to comfort him, wrapping her arms around his moth-eaten sweater and holding his frail, shaking body. He forgot his prejudice for those few brief moments, suspending it for the comfort of a warm embrace. Mrs. O'Neil rocked ferociously in her chair, blissfully unaware of her son's demise—or much else in the real world. A knife had been found on Vithu's body that tested positive for William's blood, but Conley withheld that bit of news. Parents rarely sought justice or closure when they learned of a child's murder. That small comfort came later.

Conley closed Simon's front door and descended the porch steps. The crying inside was muffled now and the silhouettes of Sage and William's parents moved behind the window sheers like ghosts.

He drove back to the marina, window down. Spring had rejuvenated Ocean Park. Trees were in blossom, perfuming the air, and the day was sublime and hopeful—a stark contrast to the misery he'd just left. Good day to take the cabin cruiser out and christen the new boating season.

Thompson's Mercedes sat in the marina parking lot. When he parked next to her, she looked up and smiled. She wore no makeup, but it had done her a disservice anyway, hiding her unblemished face and sparkling eyes.

"Hey, Conley," she said, getting out and reaching into the back seat of her car. "I've got something for you."

She handed him an album, its cover decorated with oriental shapes and symbols painted in pagan colors. He ran his hand over the leather and resisted opening it.

"Beautiful. Not here, Thompson. Inside. I could use some beauty today."

He led her down the dock ramp and held the book as she climbed onto the deck of his boat. Inside, he made coffee and they sat at the galley table. She opened the book—and he lost his breath.

A sketch of William O'Neil looked him in the eye. The tilt of his friend's strong jaw and confident smile were captured perfectly. A full-size drawing of William was next to it. He looked ten feet tall, muscles rippling, one giant hand closed in a fist, the other open, as big as a catcher's mitt.

Power and resolve.

He turned the album so they both could see. "Looks like Sage's work."

"Channary gave it to me before she left. She and Sage drew them in the safe house."

He considered that collaboration and smiled— Sage's wisdom and talent and Channary's innocence and intuition.

Lloyd Kendricks' portrait was on the next page, laughing. Lloyd's bad eye looked more like a gift than a deformity, a portal to his goodness and humor.

Sheila murmured his name, not to identify him—the likeness was unmistakable—but out of affection.

Next page.

Stefanos—his serious expression seemed to disapprove of being made into a drawing.

Mazzarelli—smiling and jovial, a cherubic face full of mischief.

Her hand, soft as down, brushed his. She turned the page to the statue of Mary, its flowing robes drawn so well they looked three dimensional.

A cicada's high-pitched whine broke the silence, birds warbled, and a breeze rustled the tarp.

Last page.

Sage and Channary had drawn the two of them, Conley and Thompson, close together, facing each other. Their identical expressions looked—*expectant.*

"Wow," he said. "The girls have quite an imagination."

Sheila's smile faltered. Was she expecting a different response? The moment passed and he felt a tinge of regret, a feeling that visited often these days, along with a gnawing disappointment with himself.

They finished their coffee. She nodded once, straight-faced, rose and tucked the book under her arm. She'd once again become the efficient social worker he'd first met. He held the door open for her and helped her onto the dock.

"Thanks for everything, Sheila. Nice job." He offered a handshake and regretted it immediately. The gesture seemed demeaning after all they'd been through. The investigation into Victor Rodriguez's murder had turned into horror and heartache, and the memories of the places it had taken them—dank basements, dangerous bars, The Paladin—were haunting.

She stared at the hand and frowned. "One more thing."

She pulled a photo from her bag and showed him. Channary stood between an old woman and a man.

"Channary sent this. We did it, Matt. She found her mother and brother."

Conley studied the picture. The woman was stoic and frail, and the brother looked proud and handsome, despite a distinctive half-moon scar that marred his youthful face. Channary's ever-present smile shone brightly—all was finally right with her world.

Suddenly Thompson tucked the photo into the sketchbook and handed it to him. "Open this once in a while," she said, her glistening eyes fixed on the cover. "They say art's good for the soul."

Chapter 45

April's weather kept improving, a warm, fragrant breath. Lisa won the special congressional election in a landslide and the *Ocean Park Gazette* published a front-page photo of the victory party. Hector Diaz's crimes had been fodder for the tabloids for weeks, a new horror revealed every day. As a result, she'd run uncontested, touted as the moral candidate. Conley smiled at the irony. She and Bill McNulty were embracing in the picture, streamers on their shoulders, delirious staffers applauding all around. At least someone was happy. The hug looked platonic enough, like a teammate's embrace. In two days their divorce would be finalized, though Lisa hadn't bothered to wait. Funny how few people ever knew the truth behind a news story.

He checked his watch, folded the paper, and dressed for church. The drive to St. Margaret's took him down winding, tree-lined streets, past cookie-cutter neighborhoods with neat houses and trimmed lawns. He parked in the crowded lot next to St. Margaret's Chapel, in the shadow of the big main church. The chapel was standing room only.

Familiar faces lined the pews. Most of the congregation of St. Ambrose was there, listening to Father McCarrick's sermon on the power of faith and the joy of forgiveness. The pulpit was modest and he was barely visible, just a voice from the altar.

After Mass, Father stood on the sun-soaked steps and greeted his flock. He smiled, nodded, shook hands, kissed babies, stood on his toes to hug matrons. When the crowd finally dissipated, Conley joined him.

"Finally found your way to the 'burbs, Matt. About time."

"Nice sermon, Father."

"If the back rows had stayed awake, I might believe you."

"How's the new rectory?"

McCarrick shrugged. "Sharing isn't easy. Mrs. Blodgett is complaining about the kitchen and she doesn't like Father Starrett's housekeeper."

"Shocker. How's everything else?"

"Metza Metz." He rotated his hand back and forth. "Crowd's been good. St. Amby's whole congregation is here."

"Okay, so what's the problem?"

McCarrick's voice raised an octave and his finger pointed at the big-domed church on the other side of the lot. "St. Margaret's crew barely makes a dent in that big ark of a church. I'd bet a jug of wine we're beating that crowd. Maybe a trade's in order."

"Father, I don't like the sound of this."

"Well, it only makes sense we switch places—for the good of the Archdiocese."

"Don't start."

He closed his eyes. "Wasn't my idea, Matt. Mrs. Blodgett made the observation. You know how she picks up that sort of thing."

"Remember, you're a guest at St. Margaret's. Be thankful for what you've been given."

"Matt, I'm being thankful…but practical too."

The last car left the parking lot. A traffic cop in a fluorescent vest was collecting orange cones. Conley held up two fingers.

"Peace, Father McCarrick."

Father sighed, lifted his cassock over his head, and smoothed his hair with his palms.

"Ah, yes, Matt. Peace it is."

****

Spring had brought an unusual calm to Ocean Park. The Gang Unit got a tip that the Asian Boyz were stockpiling guns, drugs, and cash in order to grow the drug trade, and Stefanos decided to check it out. Experience had taught him that tranquility was a gift that needed nurturing.

State troopers gathered the boys on the porch of their River Street home. They sat cross-legged on the deck, their dark, puzzled eyes staring at their captors. Conley called them into the hallway one by one for questioning while Stefanos and Mazzarelli searched. The boys denied the drug rumors and cursed Vithu for the carnage that had visited Ocean Park. His death had dissolved their fear and unbridled their hatred for him.

Mazzarelli clopped down the steep staircase holding a cardboard box that contained baggies of marijuana, a broken zip gun, and a bottle of homemade rice wine. He gave his report to Stefanos at the landing.

"Nothing, Captain."

"You searched everywhere?"

"All except the prayer room."

"I'm done too," Conley said. "I think we got a bad tip."

Stefanos sighed. "Okay, let 'em go, Conley. You

and I will toss the prayer room."

The room was painted in a riotous purple. Paper prayer flags were strung around the walls on clotheslines. Candles burned, tendrils of smoke rising. Ceramic figures lined narrow tables—offerings to Buddha—along with jewelry, macramé, and knick knacks. The puffy-cheeked Buddha smiled at it all, his golden face content.

Weren't many places to search. Conley was kneeling, checking the undersides of the prayer benches when a melancholy seized him. Blame it on the memory of Lloyd preaching in that same room, or his haunting voice—which had begun to visit often. The sadness prompted a question, which he regretted as soon as it left his mouth.

"Do you pray, Captain?"

Stefanos was inspecting the offerings, lifting statues, turning them over. He separated a collection of nesting dolls and looked inside. Had he heard the question? Conley decided he hadn't, and was glad. He wouldn't ask again.

"Nothing here," Stefanos said and returned a bracelet to the card table. His eye caught sight of a long knife with a ceramic handle, and he picked it up. One side of the blade was serrated, the other curved and sharp as a razor. The handle was covered with ornate, curling snakes.

"I pray every day," Stefanos said suddenly. Sunlight poured in through the painted windows and played off the blade. "I pray for Lloyd, for Madie and her kids, and those that are special in my life. Then I pray for me."

He laid the knife down, walked out of the room,

and looked over his shoulder.

"Time to go, Detective Conley. Our work here is done."

Chapter 46

Conley poured a cup of coffee and sat in the galley. The portholes were being lashed with a freak late-season snowstorm. Warmth and darkness made the cabin feel like a womb. He sat in the galley, opened the sketchbook Thompson had given him, and flipped the pages. They'd been through so much together—tragedy, heartache, justice and injustice. He bowed his head and reflected on how blessed he was to know each and every one.

Lloyd, Stefanos, Mazzarelli...Thompson.

The dock bell rang outside, a crisp clang muffled by the howling wind and snow. He crossed the deck and undid the transom zipper on the boat cover. Mazzarelli stood, shivering, his gloved hand still on the bell line. His entire body was caked with snow. Conley waved him inside.

"Boats are for summer, Conley. But it's pretty nice in here. Warm at least."

"I'm not looking for a roommate, Mazzarelli."

Mazzarelli took off his jacket and hung it on the door hook. He removed hat and gloves and laid them on the galley counter. His cheeks were rosy, eyes glassy from the cold. Conley poured him a coffee and they sat. Mazzarelli wrapped both hands around the mug before he spoke.

"We just got transferred, me and the captain. South

Shore."

"Nice. You'll be on Cape Cod for the summer."

"Right. Us and every college kid and pickpocket in Massachusetts."

"Don't be so negative, Mazzarelli."

Mazzarelli shrugged and retrieved an envelope from his coat. "Captain wanted you to have this—a letter of commendation. In case the O-P cops try to fry you again, there's always the staties."

Conley opened the envelope and read. He imagined Stefanos writing the words, sitting straight at his desk, brow knit, hand scribbling thoughtfully.

"Tell him I appreciate it."

They drank. The wind howled, a fierce shriek that rocked the boat against its bumpers.

"You doing okay, Conley? Captain told me to ask."

He smiled. "You tell the captain I'm okay. Better days are coming. That's my new motto."

Mazzarelli stood, shook into his coat and put on his hat. "Hard to imagine they'd be much worse."

"Bye, Conley. By the way, you done good." He looked around. "Yeah, this place ain't half bad, but you deserve better."

Conley walked Mazzarelli to the deck, watched him disappear into the whiteout, and returned to the galley. Mazzarelli had forgotten his gloves. Outside, the bell tolled again, insistently. He grabbed the gloves, went out again, unzippered the cover. An apparition stood in front of him, covered in snow, white as an angel.

Lisa.

Snow swirled around her. She wore a dress, no coat, and the left eye of her wet face sported a shiner.

Conley jumped to the dock and helped her onto the boat. Her skin was gelid and her teeth chattered, her soft shoulders trembled, and her breath smelled of alcohol.

The wind died down, the water stilled, the snow fell quietly. A surreal peacefulness consumed him. A peace that surpassed understanding.

He'd take it. Because she'd never left, not really.

When he opened the cabin door, she stopped and peered inside. They stood on the deck, huddled in almost total darkness.

"Is someone here?" she asked. "I thought I saw someone from our balcony."

He shook his head and led her inside. "No one. Just us, babe." He brushed snow out of her hair and tightened his arm around her shoulder. "There's just us."

A word about the author...

Mike Walsh attended Boston University, where he became a staffer for the *Daily Free Press* and earned a degree in journalism.

His first professional job was at a public relations and advertising firm, writing press releases that appeared in the *Boston Globe*, *Boston Herald*, and *New England Journal of Engineering*. He later became a technical writer, writing and editing jet engine manuals for General Electric Aircraft Engines. GE relocated him to Cincinnati and Florida, where he currently resides.

He's written and studied fiction for years at BU, the University of Cincinnati, and now Jacksonville, where he won the First Coast Writers Festival short story contest and had work published in the UK's Twisted Tongue and Askew Reviews. He's an active member of the Bard Society, Florida's longest-running workshop.

His five novels and dozens of short stories, most of them richly-layered mysteries, take place in New England.

Mike and his wife Jean live in Florida with their three boys.

Printed in the USA
CPSIA information can be obtained
at www.ICGtesting.com
LVHW012142020624
782073LV00025B/620